COMPANY SPOOK

COMPANY SPOOK

RONALD WEBER

A Joan Kahn BOOK

ST. MARTIN'S PRESS • NEW YORK

COMPANY SPOOK. Copyright © 1986 by Ronald Weber. All rights reserved. Printed in the United States of America. No part of this book may be used or reproduced in any manner whatsoever without written permission except in the case of brief quotations embodied in critical articles or reviews. For information, address St. Martin's Press, 175 Fifth Avenue, New York, N.Y. 10010.

Design by Janet Tingey

Copyedited by Michael Cain

Library of Congress Cataloging-in-Publication Data

Weber, Ronald, 1934–
   Company spook.

"A Joan Kahn book."
I. Title.
PS3573.E225C6   1986   813'.54   85–25148
ISBN 0-312-15326-0

First Edition

10 9 8 7 6 5 4 3 2 1

. . . and that was nearly the last we heard from him. There still were numerous loose ends to settle, but our several attempts to make contact with him all failed. He was, we knew, still in town and still performing his bureaucratic duties. When we chanced to meet in one of the corridors of power he gave no sign of recognition; he did not even favor us with that cold stare, a mixture of fear, frustration, and anger, with which we were greeted now in the rapidly crumbling executive branch of government. When at last the president resigned and took his pardon into bitter exile, Deep Well disappeared as well. In the great personnel shuffle of the new administration his absence was scarcely noticed; indeed, we suspected it was noticed by none but ourselves. That of course would be the way he wished it. He had not sought notoriety or fame; he had chosen to work behind the scenes, cloaked in obscurity, and from motives we do not pretend to fathom. The service he had performed for his country was immense, but he sought no tangible reward. Our last contact with him came in the form of a brief note written on White House stationery but folded into a plain white envelope, bearing neither stamp nor postmark, that appeared one morning at the Globe. *It said: "I have gone west, far toward the setting sun. If you need me, don't bother to look. If I need you, which is hard to imagine, you'll know it." The note was signed "James Fenimore Cooper."*

—from The Potomac Affair

COMPANY SPOOK

1

"You said?"

Walker turned the page back, then looked up. A thin redhead with a tray of dirty dishes, one of the clean-up detail, was across the table. Gray uniform. Middle-aged. He tried to remember if he'd seen her before in Sholl's Colonial.

"I said what, you said it again."

Walker tried a smile but the woman's face didn't change. She was staring at him, not the paper. He was almost certain she was new.

"So you want something or not?"

"Sorry," he said.

She waited, a middle-aged female busboy with a tray of breakfast dishes balanced on a hard jutting hip. Maybe she was.

"Just talking to myself."

"The paper, you mean?"

"No."

The redhead shrugged then and left him. He watched until she passed through a swinging door into the kitchen area. My God, he thought. I'm jumpy already. Suspicious. Talking to myself.

He turned the *Times* back to page twenty and looked again. He wasn't seeing things. He wasn't making it up, dreaming. The signal was there. He'd been following Bernie Steele's story on the California Connection deep within the paper when he saw it. The pages covered the remains of an English muffin and a cold pot of tea and he was leaning into them, trying to follow Steele's wandering prose. Steele had been a decent writer once, but the more he hounded Walker the more he wrote like him. Poorly, it was said. Walker's position was anyone could write a story; the trick was getting it. He hadn't heard of any Pulitzers going for style. Steele had learned that. He wrote just like Walker now.

The page number had been circled in red with a felt-tip pen. In the lower left corner of the page was the clock, hands set at one-thirty. If it meant A.M. it was Kane's accustomed hour. When he remembered that was when Walker began talking to himself.

He turned the page back again and looked over the cafeteria.

The thin redhead was clearing tables across the room. Paying no attention to him. Maybe not. The breakfast rush was over and only a few customers were still in the place, readers absorbed in the morning papers, the Washington addiction. He kept coming to Sholl's Colonial on Connecticut because he was left alone here. He was just someone who came late in the morning to read the papers. There were few places like it in town. If it was a matter of choice he'd choose the coffee shop of the Madison; but every tourist in town knew it was a press haunt. Every guidebook to the town said so. If he went to the Madison some couple from Iowa would want his autograph.

He was a town attraction. He was like the *Globe* building and the Potomac complex. We're up there, Bickel used to say, with Kissinger and Kennedy and the Vietnam Memorial. They'll forget, Walker had told him. But they hadn't yet. Bickel had said to hell with it and gone to New York and lost himself in the crowd. The thing about Sholl's was it wasn't the sort of place a town attraction was expected to frequent. At certain times of day flocks of tourists swept down on the place for a cheap meal, but they never thought to look for a famous journalist. In Sholl's he was ignored.

Walker turned the page back and examined the signal. It looked like the real thing, but it had been a long time. It had even been a long time since the phony signals.

For a while every *Times* dropped at his door had had the circled page number and clock. Friends, cranks, jealous colleagues, God knew who else joined in the game, duplicating the signal he and Bickel had unwisely revealed in the book about the Potomac affair. They had altered most of Kane's signals and most of everything else, but this they had left right. The mistake had finally caused Walker to change apartments, a change made possible by money from the book and the film that followed.

He'd toyed with the idea of a new place in the Potomac complex itself. He could have picked up the former attorney general's place when its owner went off for his prison term, a plush penthouse in what was still the best apartment complex in town. But he couldn't go through with it. Bickel would have done it without thinking twice, but Walker couldn't. Traces of propriety still clung to him. He still wore suits and ties and kept on at the *Globe* and stayed off the lecture circuit and limited his television appearances to an occasional "Nightline." Instead of the attorney general's place he'd bought an apartment in a Georgetown restoration and every morning picked up a *Times* at a corner newsstand and drove a silver Mercedes to Sholl's Colonial for breakfast before getting to the *Globe*. There was some conspicuous consumption in his life now, but at least he hadn't thumbed his nose at his old victims by buying the attorney general's place.

The thing to assume was the signal was a gag. Somebody remembering. Somebody who wouldn't forget. It was the sort of gag Bickel would pull if he was back in town. His calling card, he'd think of it. Or it could be Steele. Steele, desperate as time went on, might try it, seeing how Walker would react, the redhead supplying a report. Nothing else had worked, Steele might reason, so give it a try. But if Steele did it, it was no gag. Steele was serious. And dumb as ever if he thought Walker would go for it.

The other possibility, no gag either, was Kane. Harry Kane back in town. If that was true, Walker had reason to talk to himself. The questions coming again. Among other things: How had Kane gotten to the paper, gotten to it again? The old signal in the *Times* was among a few dozen things about the Potomac affair Kane had never bothered to explain. In the book Walker had told some things about the relationship with Deep Well but had avoided more for the good reason he hadn't known any more. Which was how he preferred to keep it now. It was over, behind him. Fine with him to keep it that way. It was something that had happened to him back then. He could keep living with what he still didn't know.

Suppose he drove back to the newsstand. Nothing. The grizzled fellow who ran it would look at him like the redhead had. He wouldn't know a thing. Kane's sources had always been better protected than his own, which wasn't surprising given what Kane had behind him. Had back then. Maybe still had. Anyway, checking on the paper would be a waste of time no matter who doctored it, but especially if Harry Kane had. Walker didn't even want to think about that possibility.

He got a fresh pot of tea at the cafeteria counter, carrying the folded paper with him, and came back to the table and started again with Steele's story. He had the same stuff Walker had in the *Globe*. Arab oil money had turned up in the hands of pals of the administration by way of real estate deals in the president's home state, the idea being to buy some softening of military support for Israel. The question was how high the business reached in the administration, if it reached there at all. Steele was hinting it went all the way to the Oval Office, but neither he nor Walker had the evidence. It was turning into one of those Washington stories that suddenly go stone-cold without a lucky break. Walker, familiar with lucky breaks, wasn't expecting another.

"You mind?"

The redhead was back across his table, tray on the hard hip, staring at him again.

"The dishes, you mean?"

"You mind, I said."

He lifted the paper while she cleared the table. Then he leaned close. "Do me a favor," he said. "Tell Bernie Steele he's the dumbest sonofabitch in town."

The redhead's eyes seemed to snap back in her head.

"I'd appreciate that," Walker said.

Karen asked him, "Do you?"

"I might."

"See him anymore, I mean."

"See who?"

"You know who," Karen said. "That one in the book. Deep Well."

They sat across a glass-topped coffee table piled high with oversized art books, some painting but mostly photography. Diane Arbus. Harry Callahan. After gin and tonics in her place in Alexandria Karen would fix salad and small steaks and they would drink some cheap burgundy and later maybe go out to a movie if they didn't just forget it and go to bed. If they went to a movie they would walk to the theater, Old Town section of Alexandria, and pass on the way the former home of one of the best known Potomac figures, the only one of the president's inner circle who never went to jail, that because he testified against everyone else. A distinguished senator who had played a prominent role on the Potomac committee later bought the place. Walker always thought about that when he passed the home with Karen. It made him wonder if he'd been too scrupulous, giving up the attorney general's place.

Karen explained, "Traces of propriety cling to you."

"You keep telling me."

"It's true. It's why we get along. We're both really very proper."

Walker tried his best to look lecherous. "I hadn't noticed."

"I wasn't talking about *that*." But Karen would be blushing, a full pink-to-scarlet blush that would color her entire face and wrinkle the edges of her eyes. Walker considered it the best blush in town, and very nearly the only one.

Washington women weren't blushers. They were gloss and glitter and hard edge; they reminded him of some very sophisticated neorealist painting—terrifically turned out but not something you felt the urge to hang on the living room wall. Not something you wanted to look at first thing in the morning. He liked looking now and then—who didn't?—but he could do without the misery that came packaged in the tough, upwardly mobile, faintly Southern charm Washington specialized in. He preferred to keep it simple. The woman he had in mind had her own head, but being with her was easy, relaxing—and maybe at some point she wouldn't die at the thought of becoming a wife and mother and helpmate. The question was, were there any of that sort left? Not in Washington, he'd decided. Then he'd met Karen.

Walker said, "I was."

"*You* usually are." But Karen couldn't look at him. Only later, in the dark theater, would she reach for his hand, draw it to her, whispering, "So was I, really."

Now, across the books on the glass-topped coffee table, her face was simply pale, wheat-colored hair pulled back and clasped in a ponytail. She wasn't exactly pretty—a long angular face, rather narrowed eyes—and did nothing to try to obscure the fact. No makeup, no modish hair style, no designer clothing. A jeans-and-sweatshirt girl. A take-it-or-leave-it girl. She made Walker think of the folk singers with which New Haven had abounded in the late sixties, plain wan girls with serious eyes and high pure voices that could break your heart. He'd fallen in love with them left and right.

Walker asked her, "Why do you want to know?"

"I just thought about it, I guess."

"It's odd."

"I remember," Karen said. "I saw your book at Garfinckel's this afternoon. A paperback copy. It just struck me."

"It's still odd."

She was looking at him, puzzled now.

"It came up this morning, too."

"Someone else asked about Deep Well?"

"Not exactly."

Karen went to the kitchen for fresh drinks and Walker leaned back into a flowered sofa, thinking about her. One of the things he liked was she never asked about his work. She didn't seem to care about it. She had her work, he had his; when they were together there were other things. He'd asked her once to move in with him and she had said no. The work they had to do, it would be too complicated. Maybe sometime, she'd said, but not now. When they went out, not often, she didn't need to be seen in his company, turning heads, ending up an item in a gossip column. Her idea of a big night was a movie or a drive in the Mercedes to the Maryland shore and a seafood platter and beer at some nondescript beach place. About his past work, the glory days, she had no curiosity at all. She seemed to know without his saying anything that he wanted to be an ordinary reporter again. He didn't want to keep reliving the past. There were enough in town who did. They did something once, were in the right place at the right time once in their lives, and clung to it forever. If a reporter did that, Walker knew, he was dead.

"So do you?"

"Do I what?"

She handed his drink across the coffee table. "What we're talking about. See Deep Well anymore?"

"You really want to know?"

She seemed to think about that. "No. But since I brought it up."

Walker shook his head. "The life of dark intrigue is all behind me."

"Good," Karen said, and brought her drink to the sofa beside him. "I can't imagine you ever involved in that anyway."

Later, in the darkness, she slid toward him, curving herself into his back, apologizing.

"For what?"

"For not minding my own business."

"About what?"

"Look," she said. "I shouldn't have asked."

"Ask all you want," he said, and turned until he was facing her. With his free hand he encircled her and then traced a line the length of her spine.

"And you wouldn't answer, would you?"
"Probably not."
"I don't want you to."
"I know that."
"Really," she said. "I'm sorry."
"Only words," he said. "Prove it."

▪ 3 ▪

It was there again—and with an addition now.

When the *Times* was passed in the Mercedes window Walker went through the pages until he got there, page twenty, curious only, just wondering about it. The page number was circled with a red felt-tip pen; in the lower left corner was the clock, hands set at one-thirty. Beneath the clock now was a phone number. Suburban listing.

He started to say something to the grizzled vendor, then changed his mind. The same guy gave him a paper every morning, a cold stub of cigar stuck in a square face. Maybe the same cigar. The guy never changed expression, never gave an indication he remembered Walker from one day to the next. He took the money and waited for the next car to pull to the curb.

There were two possibilities: the vendor knew he was giving Walker a doctored paper, or it was planted in the stack, arranged to coincide with Walker's arrival. It had to be the first, but if Kane was involved you couldn't be certain. Kane's way was to make it mysterious when something simple would do—

a simple phone call, for one thing. But Kane would take it for granted Walker's phone was still tapped, his mail monitored; he would figure everything was still the same. Kane proceeded from the assumption that what could happen was happening.

"Keeps you functioning," he used to say. As far as Walker knew, Harry Kane was still functioning. Out there somewhere.

He turned to look again at the vendor but a car behind him had started honking. It didn't matter. He wouldn't learn anything; he never had. He raised the car window and drove into town, following heavy traffic along M Street, trying not to think about it. If he had to think, the best thing to think was the same: it was an old leftover gag. If he called the number he'd get Bickel wanting to meet for drinks at the Sheraton-Carlton. Except Bickel wouldn't be at a number in the suburbs. Bickel wasn't the suburban type.

Walker found himself searching the rearview mirror, searching for whatever might be there. He was thinking himself into doing it the old way. Kane's way. "Be prepared," Kane always said. He also said, "All you lose is time. Your ass you might save."

At an Exxon station across from the Potomac complex he left the Mercedes to be lubricated and began walking, taking his time in the morning heat, going up through Foggy Bottom toward Lafayette Square. When he could feel the sweat building under his shirt he stopped at a coffee shop with conditioned air and a good view of the street. Nothing. Nothing but government types and George Washington University types and tourist types.

When he left the place he began walking again, taking a zigzag route now, keeping it slow, looking around. He made several blocks, then, reasonably certain he hadn't seen the same car or person, he took a cab over to the Smithsonian.

There he changed cabs and came back across town to the Capitol Hilton. It felt silly, all the bother. It was silly. It was as if he was playing himself in a movie—an old movie he didn't care to see again.

From the bank of pay phones he had a view of the lobby. Lots of convention types with plastic name badges. Lots of noise. He opened the *Times* again and got the number. There was only a single ring before the phone was lifted. That was when he knew. It was an old movie all right. It was one he knew by heart. He didn't need Kane's voice to tell him.

Walker put a finger in his ear, blotting out the lobby sounds. He said, "I'm doing a television survey. Could I have a few moments of your time?"

There was some hesitation, Kane listening. Then he said, "Leave your number. I'll get back in fifteen minutes."

As soon as Walker read off the number the connection was broken. He replaced the receiver and waited, sweating still despite the chilled air, looking back over his shoulder at the clock above the registration desk. One of those without numbers. He still didn't want to think about it. It wasn't a leftover gag; that much he knew. As soon as the phone was answered, one ring, he'd known. It was Kane's way, as if he had nothing to do but sit by the phone, waiting. It was the old movie all over again. But he didn't know anything more. He didn't want to think about it until he knew more than that. He watched the clock without numbers and tried to think about nothing.

The call came on time. That was Kane's way, too. "What took so goddamn long?" he demanded.

"Sorry, Harry."

"I sat on my ass waiting for you."

"I thought it was a gag."

"Still?"

Walker admitted it had been a while. Behind him he could

feel people gathering, and when he glanced over his shoulder he saw a group of conventioneers looking at him, trying to figure out who he was. The old joke came to him: "Weren't you that guy Walker?" It was a group from Iowa probably. He could be in trouble soon, a Washington celebrity cornered. But the Hilton was the kind of place Kane had always wanted. You talk to me on the phone, he'd said, make it public. Let me hear the background. Walker had said something then about trust. Sure, Kane said. But between friends no surprises.

"I thought it might be Bickel," Walker said. He felt surprisingly calm, he realized. Harry Kane was back in town and they were talking on the phone and it wasn't bothering him. He was thinking more about the conventioneers from Iowa. Maybe that was a way of not letting it bother him, thinking about them rather than about why Kane was back. Why he'd sent the signal again. Why they were on the phone again. Why they were back in the old movie.

"Bickel's back in town?"

"Then it could have been Steele."

"Bernie?" Kane said. "He's still pushing you?"

Kane had switched phones. Another part of the old routine. Like the newspaper. There was background noise on his end now, a low humming machine sound and people talking. Another public place. He'd switched voices, too. Crisp at first and now relaxed, bantering. Two old friends catching up. "He can't come up with anything," Walker said, "so he follows me around. Looking for you."

"Still?" Then Kane was laughing. "The glory boys never change. The missiles go off you'll worry about your leads."

"Neither do you," Walker said. "Change."

"You expected something else?"

"I wasn't expecting anything."

Kane said, "You know my motto. Be prepared."

"Okay, Harry," Walker said. "It was my mistake. I should have known it was you. I should have come."

"As long as you see it."

"I do, Harry."

"So tell me about Steele."

They were back in the movie and playing the game as if nothing had changed. It was Kane's way, turning it on and off, give a little and withhold more, nothing ever straightforward. You played the game his way or you didn't play. He'd get to it, what it was, when it suited him. The name, Deep Well, had never fit right. It was dreamed up by one of the *Globe* editors and Walker and Bickel had used it in the book. The name implied Kane had gushed out the story, whereas it came drop by drop, with long empty stretches in between, with arid times in between when Kane quit the game and stepped out of the movie and there was nothing going on. It had to be that way, he said. He'd confirm what Walker and Bickel had learned or guessed. He had to protect himself, he said. That was another thing Walker never understood—the risks Kane had run. But that was never the whole story, the risks; Kane would have played the game anyway. He would have played for sheer pleasure in the struggle. There was only one way the code name had ever fit: Harry Kane had a hell of a lot of information.

"There's nothing to tell," Walker said. "Bernie doesn't like being the Avis of Washington reporters."

"So now you're after the California boys."

Walker said, "You've been reading the papers, Harry."

"Who doesn't?"

"Bernie copies me and I copy him. Then he chases me around hunting for you." Behind him Walker could hear the convention types whispering. But they were keeping their distance; they weren't certain yet.

Kane said, "Sounds like you guys need a good source."

"Know one?"

"I might."

Was that it? The California Connection? Walker felt the calm escape, a balloon gone flat. He rubbed a moist hand along his suit coat, drying it, steadying himself. A vein began pulsing over his eyes. If that was it, Kane tossing him a new bone, then he wanted time to think. He wanted to consider what he was getting into. Maybe once was enough. Maybe after he thought about it he'd tell Kane to get somebody else. Get Bernie Steele if he wanted to risk it. Steele wanted to ride the top of the hills, let him know how it was up there. In any case, he wanted time to think. Then Kane pulled back the bone.

"But not now," Kane said. He'd switched the tone back, too; crisp now, hurried. "We've got old business to attend to."

"*We*, Harry?"

Kane ignored him. "Do it the old way."

"Because of Steele?"

"No," Kane said before breaking the connection. "More than Steele."

Walker waited as long as he could, eyes closed, sweat oozing through his shirt, holding the receiver still, letting the movie run out for the time being. Then he replaced the receiver and turned to face the circle of admirers.

4

Martha was asleep.

She was curled on a slender hip, yellow hair hugging her head, one breast visible beneath hard athletic shoulders poking against the sheet. Looking at her, Kane felt his age. Martha looked younger when she was asleep, making him feel all the older. He didn't resist facts, even this one. He was old enough to be Martha's father. What the hell: old enough to be her grandfather. If it meant he ought to feel guilt, he didn't. More a blessing. Accommodating young women weren't standing in line to move in with grandfathers.

He'd told her he was going jogging. She said, "Sure, Harry," and sat up in bed to kiss him, the sheet sliding to her waist. She took everything as normal: his age, the odd facts that he did no work and lived in a mobile home and went jogging in the middle of the night. Didn't everybody? If he asked her to join him, she would; if he didn't mention it, neither would she.

It was how he met Martha, jogging one night around the Federal mall. He'd taken the turn in front of the Capitol and was heading back along Jefferson Drive toward the Smithsonian when she fell in with him. She was a graduate student in history, out at Maryland in College Park; she said she liked to run in history's presence. That was okay with Kane. He liked talking history, and when they were on Constitution behind the Ellipse, looking up toward the White House and the

Old Executive Office Building, he had things to tell her she didn't know. Little things. Footnotes to history.

Martha gazed at him and said, "Hey, you know a lot."

"I used to know more," Kane said, and let it go at that.

As a runner Martha was marathon class. Kane wasn't up to that; he was still new to the whole thing. But he liked the companionship on a run, especially at night when it was almost cool and traffic was down and the lighted buildings and monuments along the Mall broke up the distances and they could talk back and forth. He ran then without realizing it. He didn't mind the companionship in other ways, either.

Kane returned her kiss and then fell back into the bed, Martha holding him like a vise. Regrettably, he had to work himself free.

"Another time," he promised.

"Sure, Harry," Martha said, and dropped off to sleep again.

Kane dressed in blue shorts and a jersey with orange glow tape Martha had put on the back, white knee socks to help cover an old man's thin legs, and New Balance running shoes. When he eased from the tiny bedroom he brought along a nylon backpack. In the kitchen he wrapped a fresh bottle of Jameson in a towel and placed it in the backpack with two plastic glasses. In the book Walker had said it was Scotch, but it had always been Irish. He gave him some credit: he'd managed to cover up most things. Kane adjusted the pack on his back until it felt comfortable, then switched off the lights and opened the door. A mobile home was a good place to live, among the best he'd found, but there was no way to open a door without the walls shuddering. He listened until he heard Martha's measured breathing before closing the door behind him.

The place was called Forest Estates despite the fact it had no trees. At night the brawling children were gone and the mobile homes, arranged in tight semicircles on asphalt culs-de-sac, didn't seem so impermanent. At night the place seemed less like a wagon-train encampment ready to bolt for the territory. But Kane preferred the daylight look. It looked genuinely mobile then, temporary shelter for shiftless types like Harry Kane and graduate students like Martha and construction workers who came to work on government buildings and the subway and then pulled out for some other place. The new parks tried to hide the impermanence. They tried to look like miniature suburbs, with tiny clipped lawns and hanging flower baskets and decorated mailboxes and shaded streets. Kane had settled on Forest Estates as more befitting his situation. When he had to leave there would be little left behind. Except Martha. He hadn't counted on Martha when he picked out the place.

He walked through Forest Estates a while, getting loose, then began an awkward trot. The first minutes were bitter. The first minutes his legs were stiff, inflexible, like unoiled machine parts. If he worked through that without quitting he'd find his stride; he could keep it up for miles then. His endurance surprised him. Athletics, conditioning, had never been for him; he'd agreed with what the astronaut Armstrong once said, that he didn't want to spend finite heartbeats on a pavement somewhere. Then he'd become an old guy and health was a new consideration.

He'd also met Martha and keeping up with her was a consideration.

Tonight he wouldn't mind a greater distance. The first time he ran the route, checking, Martha with him, he was surprised how little distance there was. On the Washington Metro map he'd bought it looked farther. That night he'd had the map with him, stuck in the waist band of his shorts. He'd wanted to see if the place had changed before he sent the signal. Coming upon it, deserted, lit with blue light, he'd stopped in his tracks, staring at it. He'd forgotten the route, but the place startled him with familiarity. Martha had stopped running and was looking, seeing nothing but a parking garage, all raw concrete and blue light, on the edge of a cluster of dark office buildings.

She asked, "What's up, Harry?" But he was running again. As a precaution he didn't run the route with Martha again.

On the street Kane picked up his pace. He was beginning to feel better. If there was time he'd run past the garage and then circle back, getting in more time, making sure the place was clear. It was fine cover, running. It was probably the best cover he'd ever had. Besides the health benefit, it provided anonymity. You could run anywhere, day or night, and nobody paid attention. Kane had wondered before if break-in specialists had discovered the invisibility of running. If they hadn't, they would; then he'd find something else. In the meantime running was just fine. In a long pursuit of the appearance of the ordinary he'd found nothing so ordinary.

• 5 •

Footsteps clicked on the ramp, ascending, slow and out of sync. Walker paused to look over his shoulder. Kane waited in shadows, sitting crosslegged on cool concrete, his back against a low wall. He was still sweating from the run. In Washington in summer you never stopped sweating. When Walker emerged into a patch of blue light Kane called to him.

"Drink?"

Walker stiffened, then released his breath. "Christ, Harry!"

"Scare you?"

Walker pressed a hand into his stomach, working with his breathing. "Sorry," Kane said. "Forgot you're out of shape for this sort of thing."

Sitting where he was, Walker in the light, he could get a good look. His first thought was Walker hadn't changed his uniform—still a button-down shirt, sleeves rolled to the elbows, striped tie, suit coat tossed over his shoulder. A studied informality to suit the occasion. That much hadn't changed. The rest of it was the question.

The type, insofar as that went, rarely changed. Kane knew it well: small-town Presbyterian Midwest, Ivy League college, a stint in the service or Peace Corps before law school or Wall Street or a fling in journalism, ambitious but always denying it. With most newspaper wonder boys ambition was out front, a naked sword. Bickel, for instance. Bickel would have sold out the *Globe* for a good story, to say nothing of the country. Reporters like Bickel were easy to handle; as drinking partners they were an elite. But for serious business Walker was the one Kane had wanted, the one he cultivated. There was a residue of Puritan conscience left in the type. When things got difficult you could depend on them. Kane certainly knew the type. The company had recruited them left and right. Kane felt Walker might have made a decent company man himself if he hadn't got sidetracked into journalism.

When Walker could breathe again he slid down into shadow on the concrete and Kane extended his hand. Insofar as that went, Walker took it readily enough. Everything seemed the same, but the preliminaries had to be worked through. A million dollars could play hell with even a Puritan conscience. And there was the other thing. Kane opened the backpack and took out the Jameson and plastic glasses.

"An old friend."

Walker nodded and lit a cigarette. He offered the pack to Kane.

"I quit. Booze is my last vice."

Walker said, "Where's the rest of your clothes, Harry?"

"Running attire," Kane said. "I'm into that."

"You ran here tonight?"

"Right."

"How far?"

Kane said, "You've got the phone number. Check it out; you know where I live."

"I doubt that." Then Walker said, "It takes getting used to. Harry Kane a runner."

"You think I'm too old?"

"It's not your style, Harry. Not the thing for company guys."

"More some congressman from Wisconsin?"

"More like some *Globe* reporters."

"Let's drink to them," Kane said. "My favorite bastards."

It was the right note. Walker was laughing. Kane poured the plastic glasses half full of Jameson. Walker took his and relaxed against the low wall, their shoulders nearly touching. Another thing to count on with the type, beyond the sanctity of a debt, was some friendly feeling. The type believed in that. Bickel could smile and then cut your heart out, but with Walker there had to be some personal connection. Not much, but something; it couldn't be a straight business deal, plain self-interest. The type would agonize about that. If they liked you or thought they did it solved the problem. Kane had worked to nourish the feeling, some stratum of friendship beneath the edge and irritation that had to be there, too. Friendship and conscience—they went hand in hand with the type.

But strange how few in town recognized it. None of the former occupants of the White House had. They thought you did everything through pressure—apply enough, you got what you wanted. They were all power types, but power was overrated. There was never enough to get things done right. In the company the lesson was taught early. The former occupants of the White House had had to learn it through experience.

Walker sipped the Jameson, asking now, "So why are we here, Harry?"

Kane adjusted his legs on the concrete, then tasted the drink. It was the way to drink Irish, warm, no water, get the full soft dusky taste. He'd taught Walker that lesson right away. "In a hurry?" he said.

"Curious. It's been a while."

"It has," Kane said. Then he said, "Tell me about Bickel."

"Not much to tell. He's in New York, divorced again, doing some television."

"You in touch?"

"Now and then."

"He know about me yet?"

Walker turned, peering at him through the gloom on the edge of the blue light. "Bickel and I were never close. You know that."

"Things change."

"We worked the Potomac story because the paper put us together. There wasn't anything else. Bickel didn't need to know about you then. He still doesn't."

"He just fixed up the prose, old Bickel."

Walker shrugged and turned away, leaning back against the low wall. "You know all there is, Harry. I had to tell my editor. He wouldn't go ahead with an unnamed source."

"Steiner."

Walker nodded.

"And you gave old Steiner a song and dance."

"I told him you were a composite—a half-dozen middle-level staffers."

"He still believe that?"

Walker shrugged again. "We don't talk about it."

Kane asked, "Got a woman?"

Walker waited, sipping the Jameson, smoking a cigarette. Then he said, "I'm divorced. You know that, Harry."

"No woman then?"

"Nothing serious."

"Anyone I know?"

"She's a free-lance photographer. No one you know."

"You meet here?"

"Why the questions, Harry?"

"Just curious."

"She had an assignment to shoot some pictures of me for a magazine piece. I liked the way she handled it." Walker paused before going on. "I wasn't exactly eager. She could see that."

"*Simpatico*. That's nice." Then he said, "You got plans for her?"

"Not now."

"Just screwing is all?"

Walker stared at him. "How long do we keep this up, Harry?"

"Long as we have to." Kane poured out more Jameson and changed the subject. He asked what Walker had heard about him.

"What the company said. You took early retirement when the admiral did his housecleaning. A quiet life somewhere. Tending the flowers."

"I'm back now," Kane said.

"So I see." Walker adjusted his back against the wall and lit another cigarette. "How come, Harry?"

"I missed the old town."

Walker laughed.

"Why not come back?"

"No reason," Walker said. "You're the spook. You want to come back, it's your business."

"That's so."

"But if you want to keep our business under the rug, this town isn't the best place. I told you about Steele."

"Maybe I got homesick."

"Okay, Harry," Walker said. "Play it your way."

"I am," Kane said.

After a while, drinking together, quiet, Kane said, "Brought down any governments lately?"

"Not lately," Walker said.

"So what else?"

"I didn't know better," Walker said, "I'd think you didn't trust me."

"Sure I trust you."

"Like hell," Walker said. The Jameson was reaching him. Kane could feel it himself, warmth spreading, reaching down his legs. Trouble when it was time to leave. He didn't want to think about that now, running back. He wanted to think about Walker. Kane said, "Be a sport."

Walker sighed, sipped more Jameson, said, "I'm trying to be a reporter again. Get my life back to normal. I don't want to be an editor or write books or teach or run for office."

"Just like the old days."

"It's the idea."

"They made you an editor for a while," Kane said. "So I heard."

"For a while. Now I'm back to investigative stuff."

"The Californians," Kane said. "An interesting story."

"Not very."

"Your sources—not so hot, I'd say."

"I've had better."

Kane said, "You're telling me."

The truth was he'd had Harry Kane, the best goddamn source in recent history. Maybe the best goddamn source ever. He'd had someone put a ring in his nose and lead him through the entire Potomac story. Looking back, not an easy time. Reporters were said to be a cynical and suspicious lot, but in the company it was axiomatic that they were the last true believers. They wanted to believe in someone down the line who was good and true; they were always looking for the messiah. That was why they had a romance with every new president, no matter how dull or foolish. They wanted to believe. When the president finally stubbed his toe they jumped on him, rowdy disillusioned children. When reporters stumbled into genuine corruption they wrung their hands, stunned by it all. Without Harry Kane, Walker would have given up halfway through the Potomac story. The *Globe* would have tucked tail and run back to sports and gossip and new trends. As far as Kane was concerned, newspapers weren't worth a good goddamn. Neither were reporters. Pity the country if it had to depend on either. Fortunately it didn't.

Kane finished the Jameson in the plastic glass, gentle sneaky stuff, and said to Walker, "Newspapers aren't worth a good goddamn."

"You needed the *Globe,* Harry."

"It goddamn needed me, too."

"Hey," Walker said, "no argument. We needed each other."

Kane shifted his legs, stretched, then turned until he was

looking at Walker through the gloom on the edge of the blue light. One side of his mind was comfortably drunk, the other clear and untouched. "We need each other again," he told him.

Steele brought coffee and two powdered doughnuts to a table with a view of the entrance of Sholl's Colonial. He ate the doughnuts, powder drifting over his chin onto a red plaid vest, and found himself still hungry; then he remembered he'd forgotten dinner the night before, running around after Walker. He went back through the cafeteria line for two more doughnuts and a plate of scrambled eggs. With that in him he began feeling better.

In the breast pocket of his jacket he found a White Owl wedged behind a clutch of ballpoint pens. He lit it, leaned back in the chair, and edged his thumbs inside the vest, his trademark in the profession. He wore it winter and summer. He viewed it an advantage to dress distinctively; that way people remembered you. Most journalists in town, Walker included, dressed liked they were Ivy League lawyers at Justice; they all looked alike. Steele had found a red plaid vest was plenty distinctive. He blew smoke toward the ceiling and considered a story he had to write that morning, another development in the California Connection. But before that he wanted a chance at Walker. If the bastard showed.

Yesterday he hadn't. Steele had kept up the surveillance as long as he could, then tore across town for an interview with the ambassador of Saudi Arabia, thinking about Walker all the way. He had his habits down cold. Walker never missed Sholl's Colonial for breakfast, Steele keeping an eye on the place from a delicatessen across Connecticut, having coffee himself and leafing through the morning *Globe*. Steele had someone inside the cafeteria, someone to let him know if Walker had a visitor or made a call, but the broad thought she might have tipped her hand. Walker had said something to her the other day, mentioning Steele. Steele wasn't disappointed by the development; the broad had proved useless anyway. But the day after that, when Walker didn't appear at Sholl's, he figured something was up.

As soon as the interview was over he phoned one of the attendants at the apartment parking garage where Walker kept his car. "You guys got a pair of tickets to the Orioles," Steele told him, "you call me when he gets back—again when he takes off."

"It's what we get all the time," the attendant complained.

"It's what you get again. Call me."

"You never get no Redskins?"

"It's summer," Steele said. *"Baseball season."*

The attendant phoned Steele at the *Times* bureau when Walker arrived back at his place at the usual time. The second call, to Steele's apartment, came about midnight when Walker phoned down to the garage for his car. Steele rushed from his own place—high-rent district in Georgetown but a necessary investment for keeping tabs on Walker—and arrived in time to see the silver Mercedes swing down the street.

He followed the car into town, where Walker left it at an all-night parking garage on Massachusetts near Union Station and began walking, Steele at once losing sight of him in a crowd of night people. He drove around the area for better than a half hour and then tried several hotel bars, but there was no sign of Walker. Because he couldn't think of anything else to do he took the Key Bridge to Alexandria, but the lights were off in the girlfriend's place. In itself it didn't mean anything; when Walker was there the lights were usually off. But this time the car wasn't parked in front. He drove back to Walker's building in Georgetown and found a parking place a block away. It was nearly daylight and he was slumped behind the wheel when the silver Mercedes came up the street. Steele kept low, but before he turned into the parking garage Walker gave a beep on the horn.

That's what did it.

Steele knew what it was like to chase a story and end up zero. It went with the profession. It was Walker's attitude, wise-ass, that got under the skin. That someone was on his tail was no surprise; after Potomac, Walker had been fair game for every reporter in town. But the others lost interest as the years went by; only Steele stuck it out, kept coming after him. For that alone Walker owed some respect. Steele didn't expect the Deep Well thing handed him for respect, but neither was he expecting the needle from a colleague.

If you wanted to put it that way.

Walker had beaten Steele and everyone else on the Potomac story, the flat truth, but consider how he'd done it. For all the tough pieces of the story he'd relied on Deep Well, the smart-ass name for his source. Steele had worked himself blue on the story but never caught up with Walker. He was always a step behind. Later, when the book came out with the stuff about Deep Well, he knew why. All along Deep Well was spoonfeeding Walker, giving him stuff nobody else could match. Every reporter needs sources, and in a knife-in-the-back town like Washington it was no trick finding them. But Deep Well was no ordinary source. He knew all there was. As far as

Steele was concerned, and he argued the point with anyone who cared to listen at the National Press Club bar, Walker's role in the Potomac affair was no better than a stenographer's. Any kid reporter could have gotten the story that way, and in fact one had.

Steele was candid about it: getting the Deep Well story would redeem him on the Potomac affair and reestablish his position in town. He threw himself into the effort. In the book Walker and Bickel said Deep Well held a sensitive position in the executive branch, whatever the hell that meant. Everybody in town thought they had a sensitive position. But Steele checked out everyone he could think of. After the White House crowd he went through names at State, Justice, CIA, FBI, Secret Service. He kept checking until he was satisfied someone couldn't have been Deep Well. If there was a hint of possibility he challenged the person directly. He'd say, "The former secretary of state is pointing the finger at you," altering the informant depending on the person's position. "You ask him, he'll deny it. But the word is out."

During the confrontation Steele would fasten his eyes on the subject, peering through black-rimmed glasses, waiting for some revelation. He prided himself on his powers of observation; he believed few men could keep a poker face when the fat was really in the fire. It surprised him the former president had gotten away with it so long. To Steele, watching his protestations of innocence on television, sweat glistening above quivering lips, he looked like a man about to be strapped into the electric chair. He gave the whole thing away.

"I'm ready to do a story," he'd push on. "The evidence all points your way. I've got times, places. Witnesses. Now with the secretary of state . . . You want to make a statement or wait for the story?" But he got nowhere. All he got was a lot of people roaring mad and his editors saying it was time for some foreign work, maybe the Warsaw bureau? No one had broken; not even a decent lead. It was all gossip and rumor, everyone claiming innocence while wondering about everyone else. Finally Steele turned back to what he'd considered before. That Walker had fabricated the whole business. Winged it. Made up Deep Well to cover unsubstantiated stuff he'd peddled in the *Globe* and, lucky bastard, gotten away with.

In the book Walker and Bickel portrayed Deep Well as cold and precise at one meeting, relaxed and gossipy the next. The guy swung between improbable emotions. He knew everything yet passed out information by the scrap, improbable, too. They said he was calm, detached, objective, self-assured, yet the guy would only meet with Walker, and in a parking garage in the middle of nowhere in the middle of the night. At the meetings they said he liked to crack a joke and kid around and have a belt of Scotch, yet this was the same guy who was running an administration out of office. And there were descriptive sentences that, allowing for Walker's murky turn of phrase, still made no sense. "He was a student of history, and he had developed dark and philosophical attitudes toward humankind that at times diverted his attention from immediate, practical considerations." What the hell did that mean? Was Deep Well some kind of professor?

The more Steele went over it the less it rang true. Deep Well was too conveniently complex and mysterious. Fiction was written all over the story. Inventing a source wasn't an unknown practice; some of the best stories never saw the light of day otherwise. But if Steele could prove Walker had done it in this case then he could bust his balls. The boy hero of the Potomac affair . . . working a cover-up of his own.

Steele could taste the irony he'd drape over that little revelation.

*   *   *

Walker was at the table before Steele, lost in thought, noticed him.

"Waiting for me?"

"Damn right," Steele said, lurching forward.

Walker brought a tray back to the table and took the chair across from him, sitting in a strong light. Steele eyed him closely.

"If we're going to talk, wipe the powder off your chin."

Steele ignored him, demanded, "Where were you last night, wise-ass?"

"You're getting to look like a character, Bernie."

"You look like you work at Justice."

Walker spread jelly across an English muffin. Then he said, "I think I had another meeting with Deep Well."

"You bastard," Steele growled.

"You had me staked out. Where do you think I went?"

Steele admitted he'd lost the trail near Union Station.

"It's where you always lose it. When I see Deep Well I leave the car near Union Station. It's in the book."

"Forget the book," Steele said. While Walker ate his breakfast he concentrated on the eyes. Walker was sleepy was all he could tell.

"So what do you want, Bernie?"

"Where you went."

"I told you."

Steele thumped a fist on the table. "You told me nothing."

"Why this inability to believe me?"

"Why?" Steele said. "I'll tell you why. Because there's no Deep Well. That's why."

Walker sighed. "Old stuff."

"And never was," Steele added. Then he rushed out his reasons. He'd personally checked out every possibility. He'd been up and down every list. Nothing. Everyone clean. Moreover, no one who knew what Deep Well knew about the operation could hold out so long. Why *would* he hold out? He'd be a national hero. There would be a goddamn monument on the Mall. He'd be as disgracefully rich as Walker himself. In short, it made no sense. "I'll tell you what makes sense," Steele said. "That you made it up to cover your lousy ass."

"That doesn't make sense either."

"Yeah?"

"Think about it. Why would I run the risk? There was too much to lose if I got caught."

"You'd be finished. No paper would have you."

"So why would I do it?"

Steele didn't hesitate. "Because you're a dumb bastard."

"Suit yourself," Walker said, and picked up his morning *Times*.

"You know I got you, so you pull the stunt last night. You make it look like another meeting."

"It was a meeting."

"It's what I wanted you to know," Steele said. "I got it figured."

Walker didn't look up. "You're strung out, Bernie. You ought to get more rest at night."

"I'm going to expose your ass," Steele said.

"Write anything, we'll have a look at yours. Now why not go back across the street."

When Steele rose, powder and ashes drifting from his vest, Walker said, "Your lady here."

"Yeah?"

"Her manners. They're as bad as yours."

"Yeah?"

"Do yourself a favor. Save the money."

* * *

"Who *is* this?" Karen demanded when the call came in the night, but the caller plunged on without answering.

"I know all about you. You're his girlfriend."

"*Whose* girlfriend?"

"Walker, that bastard. I know every move you two make. I've got it down in black and white."

"You've been following us?"

"Look," the caller said. "I'm letting you know for your own good. It's between me and your boyfriend. But I'll let you know anyway. I'm going to expose his ass. It'll be a scandal."

"I'm going to hang up if you don't say who you are."

"I'm telling you so you don't get caught in the mess. Everybody knows him they'll wish they didn't."

"Who *are* you?"

"Remember I told you. It'll be a scandal. He'll—"

But Karen had heard enough. She slammed down the phone.

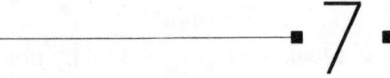

7

Maybe it was excessive, bringing him back the second time.

They were halfway through a new bottle of Jameson. That would be okay with Walker, but not another late night, not stretched out again on concrete beside a pool of blue light, not playing twenty questions in humidity that made your skin feel like a wet suit. The night before he'd gotten Walker's attention, then let him dangle for a day to see what would happen.

Nothing had—except the breakfast meeting with Bernie Steele. It was something to clarify, Walker and Steele together at Sholl's Colonial. Afterward Walker spent the day at the *Globe,* then dinner at the girlfriend's place in Alexandria. No unusual appointments or phone calls, according to Kane's information. Walker had arrived at the parking garage earlier than one-thirty, but Kane was expecting that. He beat Walker's arrival by fifteen minutes.

Irritated, Walker had asked, "You thought I was bringing the FBI?"

"I'd have known that," Kane said.

"Who then?"

Kane tried to look apologetic. "You know me. Cautious to a fault."

Then he'd gotten the new bottle and the plastic glasses out of the backpack and they'd finished half of it, leaning against the low wall, shoulders nearly touching, Walker smoking, saying nothing to each other, letting the irritation settle. Maybe it was excessive, Kane thought again. He'd almost convinced himself Walker wasn't part of the problem.

"Tell me about the money," he said now, going on with it anyway. "What's it like, being rich?"

"New apartment, new car, investment counselor. About the same otherwise."

"I've wondered about that," Kane said. "Having a bundle."

Walker lit another cigarette, his face glossy with sweat in the yellow flare, then sipped the Jameson. "It's better than not having it. That's all."

"Nice to know," Kane said. "Takes a load off my mind. Anyway, you've got the dough but your heart's desire's another big story."

"Ordinary stories will do." Then Walker said, "Not ambitious enough, Harry?"

"There are other things."

"Like running?"

"Fine thing," Kane said. "Keeps you in shape."

"For what?"

Kane refilled his plastic glass, letting the talk flow now, allowing himself the luxury of a final check. Excessive probably, but you never knew. Even with Walker's type you never knew. When you thought you did was when you were in trouble.

"In shape for the company, Harry?"

"I'm retired," Kane said. "An old fellow keeping his heart going."

"I doubt that." Then Walker said, "It must be something big to bring you back. Why would the company risk it?"

"You don't believe in homesickness? I missed talking with you in these fashionable surroundings. I missed the Washington social whirl. Intimate dinner parties in Georgetown. Luncheon with the ambassador's wife. Hunting weekends in Virginia with Pentagon brass. You miss that sort of thing in the provinces."

"It wasn't your style, Harry."

Kane shrugged. "You're right. It's for the press corps, that stuff. I lived vicariously through you guys."

Walker raised his plastic glass, a mock salute. "Same old Harry."

"You, too."

But one thing wasn't the same. Maybe only what a few years can do—that and more money than you can spend. Walker wasn't as torn up with anxieties now, torn up over what he thought of as a career, worrying he was going off the deep end with the Potomac story, hanging himself. Kane had had to hold his hand, keep pumping him up. It had made for some tense evenings in the parking garage. It was the reason he taught

Walker about Jameson, gentle sneaky stuff, courage-making stuff. Walker looked like he could relax now, with or without the Jameson. He looked like he could take his time, letting Kane lead, waiting for whatever it was. He looked like he almost had a sense of humor now.

Kane stirred on the concrete. "Take a leak?"

They went down the curving ramp and out to a rectangle of manicured lawn between the parking garage and a drive-in bank. The streets were deserted, the dead quiet magnifying their sound. When they were back Kane poured out more Jameson.

"Last one."

He was convinced enough. You never knew for sure but you had to to decide. He decided Walker was still true to what passed as journalistic ethics. A much simpler matter actually: you protected your sources or you didn't have any. You never burnt a source unless he burnt you first. But it pleased journalists to imagine they had an ethical code like real professionals. It ennobled the trade, turning gossips and PR hacks into priests and princes. Not that Kane minded. The commitment to the code of protected sources made his work possible. Without the code he wouldn't have been able to do business with Walker. Journalists never understood that; they never knew how thoroughly they aided him—him and those like him. Journalists were all children at heart; their names in print was all they asked. Walker's type was better but not different.

Kane sipped the Jameson, said, "As I was saying—"

"Saying last night."

"As I was saying last night, we may have ourselves a problem. I had a visit—before the first signal—from Sam Pearlman. I'm still not certain how he found me. I don't have a phone—the number you called is a pay phone in a laundromat."

"Not the number I called," Walker said. "The number you called back from."

"Oh?"

"Noisy background."

"My mistake. At any rate, I'm living in a mobile home—a temporary matter. A liquid situation, you might call it. But Pearlman found me."

"Why is that, Harry? Why are you back in town?"

Kane hardened his voice. "Let's keep it to this. Okay?"

"Hey," Walker said. "Keep your jersey on."

"As I was saying," Kane went on. "Pearlman found my place. I was out, playing some tennis. He left his card with Martha and asked me to call."

"Tennis, too?"

"Since I was reborn," Kane said. "Like some of our Potomac friends."

"And Martha?"

"A new friend."

Walker raised his glass, another salute. "Same old Harry."

"We're talking about Pearlman," Kane said, and kept the hardness in his voice. "Your literary agent, right?"

"Everyone's agent—all the Potomac players. Both sides."

"So what's he want with me?"

Walker sipped his Jameson, thinking. Then he said, "Fishing expedition. There's one thing left to know—the identity of Deep Well. One last book to write. One last payoff. I've got a standing offer from Sam—one million for Deep Well Revealed."

"So what's it got to do with me?"

"My guess is nothing in particular. Sam makes his offer to anyone remotely involved and hopes he'll get lucky. He's like

Steele—he goes up and down the list. He doesn't know anything for sure. He can't."

"I'm a long way down any list."

"It can't be anything else," Walker insisted. "He must be going through everyone, systematically, and he finally got to you."

"He's that persistent?"

"Where there's big money."

"Okay," Kane said. "Say you're right. How'd he know I was in town and where to find me?"

Walker shrugged. "Maybe someone recognized you. Running around in no clothes, you could get noticed that way. Maybe your new friend told someone who told someone else. Maybe you've got a leak in your other business. Sam gets around."

"Who else wants the money?"

"Still? Only Steele as far as I know. At one time every journalist in town took a crack at it. The big papers assigned teams. The newsmagazines. *Rolling Stone, National Enquirer, Playboy, Harper's,* the networks. They all tried. Brits, Germans. What they found is a simple story. Two people know. You and me. There's no story, Harry. Only guesswork."

Kane said, "Speaking of Steele. You two breakfast chums now?"

Walker said nothing. Then he lit a cigarette, looking at Kane in the yellow flare, and said, "You're going to a lot of needless work, Harry."

"Not me."

"Your people then."

"So?"

"So nothing. I told you Steele's still hounding me. He knew I was out last night—he wanted to let off steam. He caught me at Sholl's. The current fantasy is I made you up."

"And he keeps coming because he's like Pearlman?"

"It's fame with Bernie. That and money." When Kane didn't reply Walker said, "That's got to be it, Harry. Sam's on a fishing expedition."

"Okay," Kane said. "Let's assume that. Pearlman and Steele know nothing for sure. Then let's assume something else. Let's assume we've got somebody else in this with us."

A message from Karen was on the answering service. She wanted him to call when he got in.

"But I didn't mean *this* late. It's four o'clock in the morning."

Walker apologized for forgetting the time.

"Who is she?"

"She was a he. Business."

Karen said, "I almost believe you." Then she explained about the strange phone call. Someone insisting he was going to expose Walker and create a scandal. He said he was informing Karen for her own good.

"He's been *following* us."

Walker sighed and asked for a description of the voice. Then he said, "It's nothing to worry about. I know him. He's a little crazy at the moment."

"It was scary."

"If you knew him it wouldn't be."

"I just wanted to tell you," Karen said. "In case it was important."

"It isn't," Walker said, pleased she didn't ask for more explanations, didn't go on about it. He was on the down side of the Jameson now, fit for a minimum of questions and then bed.

"I'm sorry if I sounded excited."

"I like you to sound that way."

"Oh, you know what I mean." Then she said, "Should I ask who you were out with so late?"

"You wouldn't believe me if I told you."

"I might."

"You wouldn't," he said. "Believe me."

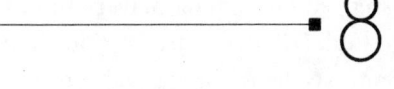

Given his build, short and wiry but quick afoot, tennis was the one game Sam Pearlman could play with skill. He was a tactician as a player, moving larger and lumbering opponents around with well-placed shots until he had them worn down, red in the face and gasping, at which point he grinned across the net, adjusted thick and rimless spectacles beneath a hairless head, and began placing his shots with even greater finesse. He kept it up until they begged for mercy. Pearlman took pleasure as well in the garb of the courts, the shorts and sweaters and monogrammed polo shirts, though for his own wardrobe he preferred a little color, some yellow and pale blue and tangerine, in place of the standard white.

But he wasn't so wrapped up in the game that he neglected business. Ordinarily he didn't mix the two; you did that you could lose concentration. Pearlman prided himself on his concentration. Most people wandered in the head, they trailed off in the clouds. Pearlman's mind, on the other hand, was sharp as a dollar when he worked at it. It was his advantage. But when Harry Kane called him he said to meet at some public courts in Silver Springs and Pearlman went along with the guy. Flexibility was another thing he prided himself on. You had the two, concentration and flexibility, you had all you needed in his business. When the little blonde, thin as a pole, told him the guy was playing tennis, he mentioned his own interest in the game, a casual remark, but it had gotten back to the guy. He'd picked it up. Pearlman made a mental note to the effect Kane had some concentration, too.

Pearlman caused the first ripple of attention around the courts when he pulled into the cinder parking lot in a black Jaguar, the second when he stepped out among players in cut-off jeans and T-shirts in an Eddie Bauer warm-up outfit of burnt orange. They were on a dusty bench now, waiting for a court to open up. Kane said he hadn't counted on the delay.

"I wasn't expecting no country club," Pearlman told him.

"Good."

Pearlman had been trying to size the guy up, get some handle on him. He didn't know him from Adam. "You an old-time player, Mr. Kane?"

"Harry."

"Sam here."

"As a matter of fact," Kane said, "I'm new to the game."

"Since you left the White House?"

Kane nodded. "For the old heart—give it a workout."

"Me," Pearlman said, "I started on courts like these. Worse even."

"I'm looking forward to playing with you," Kane said. "You're a bit of an expert, I hear."

Pearlman dismissed the compliment by removing his glasses and vigorously polishing the lenses with a monogrammed handkerchief. "You've been checking, Harry."

"Not really."

"Guy shows up at your door out of the blue, you want to know about him. I'd do the same."

"In that case," Kane said, "you might tell me how you found me."

"In the trailer place?"

Kane waited for him to go on.

Pearlman replaced the glasses and observed the guy. "So while we wait we can maybe talk some business. That okay, Harry?" What he saw was a skinny, tanned, older guy, middle sixties maybe, with gray hair bunched out on the sides of his head and a few strands laid between. He didn't look promising. He looked like a million other guys. The fact was Kane was near the bottom of Pearlman's list, a long shot or worse. But that's where concentration came in. Everything said pass the guy up, keep on the lookout elsewhere. He had to remind himself that in business you couldn't be too careful; you kept playing your cards, see what developed. Who could have figured the former press secretary for a sex novel? One of the Senate guys, Nebraska or somewhere, for a hot religious item? With big names all Pearlman needed was to flash some dollar signs and the books rolled in, but other things came by beating the bushes, saying around, "I'm Sam Pearlman, the agent. Maybe we can do some business." Most of the time he came up empty. Now and then you wouldn't believe.

What nobody would believe was the Deep Well thing. He put himself to sleep nights imagining it. There might be a lunch with some guys like Siegelman at Norton and he'd say, offhand, third martini, "I maybe got a little something of interest, Howard. A little something on the Deep Well thing. Yeah, you heard right. *Deep Well.*" Other nights he did the book with an auction, everybody's tongue hanging out while the figure went through the ceiling. What a pleasure handling that little item! The anticipation was enough to get him out to nowhere places like Silver Springs, picking up splinters on a bench with an old guy bottom of his list, looking at kids fool around the courts.

His concentration good as he could get it, Pearlman said to the guy, "So maybe we could start with what you did in the White House."

"I'm sure you know, Sam."

"Could be. But say anyway."

"I worked for the president's staff. My cubicle was in the basement."

"And you did what in the cubicle, Harry?"

"Paper specialist. I coordinated the memos. Internal Communications was the name."

"Big job, huh?"

"Small, actually. But every organization needs a paper specialist, see that it all flows properly. Think of the number of memos that circulate in the White House in a single day."

"I'm trying."

"Hundreds. They all have to be routed. Then there's filing."

"You sent some up to the president, Harry?"

"That was part of the job, knowing where they went. Some had political implications, they went certain places. Security implications, other places. A few went to the president. You had to know."

"How'd you learn the trade, Harry?"

The guy smiled, big toothy grin. "Now that I'm sure you know, Sam."

"So say anyway."

"I had the same job with the company for many years. I saw to the paper. Central Reference Service it was called."

"What section was that, you don't mind me asking."

"Operations."

Pearlman's eyebrows edged above his glasses. "Operations, huh?"

"I was there a long time. Thirty years. When the White House needed an experienced paper man, I went on loan."

"The company," Pearlman mused. "Operations. Hot stuff, Harry."

Kane shrugged. "So's the White House. Not everybody in the company's a spook, Sam. In fact, I understand very few are. I'm not sure I ever met one."

Pearlman examined two young guys playing off to the side. He watched until he was satisfied he could handle either one. "With your position, Harry, you maybe could have been Deep Well."

The guy smiled again, showing his teeth again. "So that's what it's about. You had me wondering, Sam. A literary agent wanting to talk to me."

"All those memos, you could have learned some stuff."

"You really had me wondering."

"Inside stuff, going right through your hands. Some of it could have stuck, Harry."

"Sorry to disappoint you, Sam. Most of the memos I saw were about new paint for the johns."

"You could have learned some secret stuff," Pearlman went on. "Maybe passed it on. You know Walker, by the way?"

Kane appeared to reflect. "The one who wrote the book about Deep Well? I may have seen him around the press room."

Harry Kane was no player. Remember his age, his conditioning wasn't so bad. But the guy had no swing. He went for the ball like a baseball, Pearlman popping strikes past him like Nolan Ryan. He kept it up for twenty minutes, then let the guy call it quits. He came around the net dripping sweat and offering compliments on Pearlman's game.

"You're tough, Sam. Like they say."

"So-so," Pearlman agreed, and tucked his racket under a hairy arm.

"Sorry I couldn't give you more competition."

"Maybe your heart's not in it, Harry."

"You think that's the problem?" Kane laughed but admitted Pearlman had a point. He didn't have a real dedication to the game. He liked the exercise and the life of the courts, the ambience, if Pearlman knew what he meant. He liked the sun and the steamy asphalt and the way kids lounged on the benches between games.

"You got a little poet in you, Harry."

Kane toweled his face and then directed Pearlman to an empty bench.

"You want to talk some more, Sam?"

Surprised, Pearlman said, "About business, you mean?"

"Why not?" Then Kane said, "Let's say I'm your man. For sake of discussion. Let's say my job down there gave me access to all the Potomac stuff. Then let's say I passed it on to the reporter you mentioned."

"Walker."

"So what good would it do you? You want a book telling the world about Deep Well, right?"

"What else?"

"But what if Deep Well turns out a nobody, a low-level bureaucratic type with a name nobody ever heard before? Who's going to care? Who's going to put down money to read about it? People want a Deep Well they already know, one of the big Potomac names. The former secretary of state, to take an example. What would be better than that?"

"Nothing," Pearlman said morosely, seeing the point.

"Or one of the president's own boys?"

"Not bad."

"Someone in his family. The son-in-law. That ever occur to you, Sam?"

"First thing."

"The wife even."

"After that."

"If I'm Deep Well, it's no good as a story."

"So maybe only historical interest," Pearlman said without conviction.

"A footnote. You interested in footnotes, Sam?"

Pearlman removed his glasses and began polishing, buying some time for what lingered of his concentration. "How come you left the White House, Harry, you don't mind my asking?"

"The new administration had its own paper man. I went back to the company."

"Back to Operations, huh?"

"Yes."

"And you did the paper there."

"Until my retirement."

"Now you got a little girl and play some tennis."

"That's it," Kane said.

Pearlman replaced the glasses and grinned at Kane. "A nice little blondie girl, Harry."

"She keeps me young."

"Yeah?" Pearlman said. "Tell me about it."

Kane walked with Pearlman back to the black Jaguar, stood by the door while Pearlman got back into the burnt-orange warmup outfit and buckled himself into a leather bucket seat. Halfheartedly, he suggested lunch to repay Kane for his trouble.

"I'd prefer something else, actually."

"So?"

"Do you suppose I could get a copy of each of the Potomac books? I believe the authors were your clients."

Pearlman squinted at Kane through the open window. "You want to read up?"

"It's my young friend. She has an interest in history."

"They're yours," Pearlman said.

"There's just one other thing," Kane said. "You didn't answer before. How did you find where I'm living, Sam?"

"The little trailer place? You keeping it secret, Harry?"

"Curiosity is all."

"I was wondering," Pearlman told him. "An old company guy in a place like that. So I go out rather than send a letter. See the place."

"I didn't write one of your books, Sam. I've got civil service retirement is all."

"That's the reason, huh?"

"How did you find out?" Kane asked him again.

Pearlman shrugged. "So what's it matter. A tip, Harry. A little note in the mail. No name."

"That must have struck you as strange. Why would anyone go to the trouble?"

Pearlman shrugged again. "You're in my business, you get stuff in the mail. People know I'm making the rounds on Deep Well. You keep them out of it, they don't mind a tip."

"It's that kind of place, all right," Kane said. "Washington."

"I'll tell you some more, Harry," Pearlman said. "I'd figured I had to pass you up. An old company guy, it wasn't worth the effort. You never find a company guy, they don't want to be found. Then I get the tip."

"Convenient," Kane said. "But sorry you wasted your time."

"It happens," Pearlman said. Then he beckoned Kane closer, summoning his concentration, watching the guy. "This stuff you said. You wouldn't be shitting me, would you, Harry?"

"I'm not your man, Sam," Kane said, and smiled at him through the window. "I wouldn't make a story."

▪ 9 ▪

"You couldn't let me know?"

The anger was genuine now. He'd waited in the parking garage half an hour, smoking and growing fretful, a touch of the old fear he'd felt back in the beginning back with him. Then he remembered another of the signals. When there was a change in plans—or when Harry Kane changed his mind or just wanted to run him around or for whatever reason he never understood—he would leave a message on a ledge near a stairway. Walker looked and found it, a wadded-up note in a dust-caked crevice with the name of a truckers' café out on the Capital Beltway near Sutland, a place they had used before.

He had to walk a half-dozen blocks back to an all-night People's Drug and call a cab to get him back to town and the parking garage near Union Station where he'd left the Mercedes. Then he had to make the trip out to Sutland. Kane, wearing chino pants and a big-flower blue-and-white Hawaiian shirt, was at a table in the rear of the place, beyond the bar and a bumper-pool table and some out-of-order video machines. His feet were propped up on a chair and he was reading a *Time* magazine, a month out of date. That's when Walker's anger became genuine. Figuring the delay, Kane had brought along some reading material.

"A phone call, Harry. It's too much to ask?"

"You forgot the signal?"

"I'm too old for these games. We both are."

"Sorry for the inconvenience." But Kane didn't sound sorry. He sounded like Harry Kane in one of his all-business moods. No playing the game now; no hide and seek. After two meetings, he said, it was time to change the routine. As a precaution. "You notice anything?"

"That I'm tired and you're sitting here reading a magazine."

"On the way is what I meant."

"I know what you meant." Walker took a chair across from Kane and lit a cigarette. Then he said, keeping his voice low, "Let's settle something, Harry. You're back in town for some reason. You're the one sticking his neck out. You want to keep Deep Well under the rug, it's not the way to do it."

"No?"

"You've got something to say to me, say it. You want to see me, give me a call."

"You don't like our old spots anymore?"

"I didn't like them then."

"As I recall," Kane said, "you were eager enough to come then. I had the impression you wanted to see me then."

"Forget it, Harry," Walker said. "That stuff's over."

Kane closed the magazine. "It's what I've been trying to tell you. It's not."

When a sleepy waitress came to the table Walker ordered a cheese on rye and draft beer. Kane had an empty plate on the table and two empty beer glasses; he was working on a third. The place hadn't changed; it was as disagreeable as ever—flimsy paneled walls, stained ceiling tile, the smell of frying oil and old cigars a permanent feature of the air. Walker removed his coat and tie but still felt overdressed. Up front were some truckers hunched over coffee and some late-shift types in jeans and dirty T-shirts killing time before facing up to the wife and kids. He noticed now the song on the juke box: Willie Nelson in a duet with another cracked, nasal voice.

"That's the case," Walker said, "should we be seen together in this garden spot?"

"It was okay before," Kane said.

"Before I wasn't a famous reporter. My picture wasn't in the papers and I wasn't on TV. I didn't have a Mercedes parked out front."

"I wouldn't worry. Even your fame has limits, and this dump is one of them."

"I'm not worrying. You're the one taking the risks."

"So you said before."

With a cigarette and then the beer and sandwich Walker began feeling better. He could look at Kane now without his anger rising. Looking at him, you could almost believe he was a factory worker putting down the beer before heading home to sleep until noon. He didn't look out of place. Except for the tan, too deep for a factory worker, and the big-flower Hawaiian shirt no factory worker would wear; but there was an attitude about him, the way he was sunk in the hard chair with his feet up on another one, that fit in. You saw him in the White House basement, you felt the same. He wore a dark suit then with vest and striped tie and had his hair trimmed every week and went around in the same noiseless way as everyone else who thought they were working at the center of earthly power. You noticed him and yet you didn't, not as a separate person. It made Walker wonder how many other roles Kane had played. Not that he expected he'd ever know—or wanted to. It was another of the things about Kane he'd never know and could leave that way.

"This a company place, Harry?" he asked, bringing up one of them anyway. He had the sleepy waitress bring him another draft, trying to relax a little. He was here now; he'd spoken his piece to Kane; he'd had some food. "It's so bad it must be. How else could it stay in business?"

When Kane didn't say anything, Walker said, "The look of your outfit, you didn't run out here."

"Too far," Kane said.

"Drive?"

"No car," Kane said. "I got a lift."

"Company car?" Walker said. "You don't mind the pun." Then he said, "You been in Hawaii, Harry? The shirt, I mean."

Kane looked down as if he hadn't noticed what he was wearing. "Vacation."

"I doubt that."

Kane shrugged, looking Walker in the eye, his all-business look now to go along with the all-business tone. "Could we get on with it? I thought it's what you wanted."

"I do."

"First point then," Kane said, and straightened in the chair. Walker had been right about Sam Pearlman. As they planned in the meeting in the parking garage, Kane had seen the agent; that was the first step, Kane had said, feeling him out before they did anything else. But as Walker had figured, Pearlman was only on a fishing expedition, and none too serious about it in Kane's case. Kane was just another name on a long list. Kane was convinced the agent had no information and no suspicions as far as he was concerned. Pearlman had just been going through the motions.

"How'd he find you, Harry?"

Kane explained that Pearlman had received an anonymous tip giving him Kane's address. Pearlman didn't seem to take that too seriously—it happened all the time, he'd said, hunting for Deep Well—and neither did Kane.

"You kidding, Harry?"

"I would," Kane said, "if I didn't know where the tip came from. I think I do."

"Where?"

Kane ignored the question. "So for the time being we assume Pearlman isn't our problem. He was just trying his luck. Bad luck, it turned out." Kane finished his beer and beckoned to the sleepy waitress for another. When she was gone, he said, "Second point. Somebody in town, not Pearlman, has suspicions about me."

"You said that before. You said somebody else was in this with us."

Kane nodded.

"A guess, Harry? Intuition? Black magic?"

Kane looked at him.

"Something's happened then?"

"Maybe."

"*Maybe?*"

"What I'm saying," Kane said, "is there's reason to believe people in town may be on to me."

"Plural, Harry? People?"

"You called them the repairmen in the book. Not a bad name. I always liked it better than Deep Well." Kane drank some beer, watching Walker. "Those people."

Walker stared back.

"It's their touch," Kane said. "You know them, you can't miss it."

After a while Walker said, "The *repairmen*, Harry?"

"They were put together to keep things functioning properly from the administration's point of view, but they missed the biggest malfunction of all. Me talking to you. That malfunction. They don't care for mistakes like that."

"But those guys went to jail."

Kane said, "Some went to jail—some of the more visible members. It was a sizeable organization in its prime. Very busy."

"So what's the point? All that stuff's over now."

Kane shook his head. "Some things are, some aren't. Those people took pride in their work, and their pride was hurt. To be precise, they were humiliated. They don't like that. They want to get even. It's as simple as that." Then Kane said, "It's possible they're still acting under orders."

"Whose?"

"Whose do you think?"

"C'mon, Harry," Walker said. "You can't believe the president is still calling the shots. He wouldn't risk it. Not with his pardon."

"I didn't mention the president," Kane said. "You did."

"If it got out," Walker said, "the country would have his head."

"So maybe they're acting on their own. Free-lancing. It doesn't matter. What matters is they're active again."

Walker lit another cigarette and said, "Let's say you're right. What do they want?"

"My ass."

"And mine?"

"Good question," Kane said. "Ordinarily no. You were doing a job. It wasn't you, it would have been someone else. On the other hand, you aren't one of their favorite people. It's something to find out."

"What else?"

"Glad you asked," Kane said.

* * *

Walker listened, understanding none of it. It was the old movie again. They were back in the past and he wasn't rich and famous and Harry Kane was telling him what to do and he understood none of it. He was back where he didn't want to be and it was happening all over again.

Kane's plan was for Walker to journey into the heartland to see the vice president. The former vice president. Kane gave the state ("Michigan somewhere") and the setting ("the woods somewhere"); the rest he left to Walker. The cover was he was doing a story on the vice president for the *Globe*. Locating the man after his years of absence from Washington would be a story in itself, but Kane suggested embellishments since, given the way the California Connection was going, Walker could use a lift ("keep your name in lights"). What was it like to live with shame, with the knowledge that history would be unforgiving? Something along that line.

"The vice president," Walker said. "Not the president."

"We know where the president is," Kane said.

"But what's the point, Harry? What's it have to do with the repairmen?"

But Kane would say no more. After Walker had seen the vice president they would meet again.

"And that's it? I do a story on him and that's it?"

"For the time being."

"What if the *Globe* doesn't want it?"

"Make them want it."

"That isn't so easy, Harry."

"It used to be."

Before he left, Walker said to Kane, "I'm doing this because I owe you one."

"More than that, I'd say."

"The point is I owe you. But not forever."

Kane smiled. "Another beer before you go?"

Walker looked down at him, the tan, the big-flower Hawaiian shirt, the smile now. Another guy drinking away the night and listening to Willie Nelson sing through his nose. You could almost believe it. "No thanks." Then he said, "You need a lift?"

"No thanks."

"Company car coming?"

"To this dump?" Kane said. "Not likely."

The former vice president was thoroughly disgraced. He had resigned his office when the financial scandal around him had mushroomed to the point of the office or jail. He'd tried to brazen it out, denying the allegations and charging envy and malice on the part of his enemies, but at length he quietly left office. For a while there were friends he could count on, those who agreed with his conservative political views and were convinced he was the victim of a liberal conspiracy, and he surfaced now and then at golf outings and yachting parties. He looked unusually well on these occasions; in the photos that appeared in the press he was relaxed, cheerful, and as impeccably groomed as ever. Finally even his closest friends found it difficult to dismiss the evidence against him and the press lost interest. There was a divorce and then bankruptcy proceedings. After that the vice president vanished into the country.

Walker's colleagues at the *Globe* had little information and less inclination to uncover more. There was a rumor the vice president was writing an exposé novel, one in which he would lash out again at his enemies and reveal the true story of his relationship with the president, but no one had bothered to check the rumor out. There was no longer any interest in the vice president. The most recent clip in the files was a small boxed story, datelined Boulder, Colorado, with a headline reading EX-VEEP'S DAUGHTER GETS LAW DEGREE. The story noted the vice president hadn't attended the commencement ceremony. But the rumor about the novel was enough.

"So how come you're looking for him?" Sam Pearlman asked when Walker phoned him.

Walker told him about the idea for a series of profiles on all the old administration people. The way he was thinking, it would be a where-are-they-now sort of thing.

"Not bad," Pearlman said. "It could sell. All those guys are out of jail now."

Walker explained he wasn't thinking about a book. Only some pieces for the paper.

"You giving up the California stuff?"

"A change of pace." To sound more convincing he added, "I feel like some travel."

"There may be something we can put together on them California guys," Pearlman mused. "After the change of pace."

"How about the vice president, Sam?"

Pearlman had it all. The vice president was in Michigan, living with a woman who had a place on a river near a town called Grayling. The woman had a post office box in the town and Pearlman had corresponded with the vice president through her. He was urging him to do a novel. "You know, a roman-à-clef thing." The vice president was desperate for money to satisfy old legal fees; Pearlman was convinced the novel would sell. "It don't have to be no good. His name on it, we got enough." After the novel, the vice president back in the public eye, there could be memoirs.

Walker asked about the woman.

"Maybe a right-wing broad, wants to be his mother. Get him back on his feet. Maybe a young chick. Who knows? She got him working is all I know. For that I'm grateful. I love her to death."

Walker thanked him for the information.

"You see him," Pearlman held him, "push the book. From you he might get inspired."

Walker said he'd do his bit for the cause of letters.

"Tell him about the guy did the religious book. He got a place in Malibu after jail."

"Count on me, Sam."

"About them profiles," Pearlman went on. "Maybe we can get together."

"We'll see, Sam."

"And don't forget them California guys, neither."

From the *Globe* Walker put in a call to a stringer in Detroit, asking for details about the woman. It took two days, but what he learned was that a Dorothy Cott Fairly, the widow of a ball-bearing manufacturer who had made a fortune in the auto industry, was spending the summer at her lodge on the Au Sable River, a trout stream in the northern part of the lower peninsula. The woman was devoted to fly fishing and had a reputation in the area for skill with a rod. Walker wondered if that was unusual, a woman interested in fly fishing, but the stringer said he'd heard it wasn't uncommon; at least people in the area didn't think it was. The stringer's information was that there was a man living with Mrs. Fairly who generally fit the description of the vice president, but no one in the area had any idea that was who he was. There was just a man out there at the lodge was all anyone knew. When Mrs. Fairly came in to Grayling to pick up her mail she came alone, and she hadn't been seen in any of the town's restaurants or taverns. It was common knowledge that Mrs. Fairly spent her summers at her lodge and fishing on the Au Sable River, and common knowledge that this summer a man was living with her, but no one in the area cared who he was. The local view was, you had her money you did what you wanted.

"She may be the one you want," the stringer said, "but no guarantee. There may be lots of women living with guys in the woods."

Walker asked about her political background.

"Her husband used to give to the Republicans. He was big with Romney. Did some business with AMC. About her I can't find out. She's no joiner."

Walker asked what Mrs. Fairly did during the rest of the year, when she wasn't fishing.

"She lives in Grosse Pointe Shores," the stringer said. "She doesn't do anything."

Walker thought again about trying to phone ahead for an appointment, but Kane had given emphatic instructions on that score. "Go. No advance notice. Show up, try to talk to him." When Walker mentioned potential delays and wasted time, Kane said in the all-business voice, "Cold turkey or not at all." His editor, Steiner, was less enthusiastic than Walker about the sudden departure and the temporary dropping of the California Connection for profiles of old administration figures happily forgotten. "That's dumb shit," he said. "Probably," Walker agreed, but tried to make a case for doing the vice president to see if the series had possibilities. "Sam Pearlman thinks it might," he said, making, he knew at once, one argument too many. "Then I know it's dumb shit," Steiner said.

But finally he gave a lame go-ahead and Walker looked up Grayling in Rand McNally.

At the last minute he asked Karen to go along. Kane wouldn't approve, and Walker usually avoided mixing business and pleasure. But in this case it didn't seem to matter; he didn't know the real purpose of the trip anyway. The work he was doing was Kane's work, whatever it happened to be. If it mattered, he could count on Karen's discretion. What mattered more was he wanted her on the trip. He wanted the companionship. With her along the prospect of wasting time up there in the woods didn't seem so bad. He might even waste more than he needed to. Thinking about it that way, forgetting Kane and thinking about Karen, put a whole new light on the trip.

"I'll need a day to clear my calendar," she said when he asked her. She thought the trip sounded like fun. When he explained he was researching a series of profiles on former administration figures, starting with the vice president, she wondered—a thought only, not pushing it—about photographs to go along with the stories. "We collaborate now," Walker said. Karen, blushing, explained, *"Professionally,* I meant." He said, "That way too if you want," and in fact it wasn't a bad idea. Words and pictures about the old Potomac players—maybe something for Sam Pearlman, maybe a kind of sequel to the Potomac book. He had to remind himself the business about profiles was the cover, Kane's idea, for a trip proposed by Kane for reasons only Kane knew. He didn't like the thought of Karen shooting pictures to no purpose. He'd have to tell her, afterward, that the series fell through. After that he'd tell her, sometime, why it did, clearing away the deception. With Karen he didn't want any deception. He wanted it clean and simple. If it began that way, it might stay that way.

11

They took an early flight from Washington National to Atlanta. There, buying tickets at the last moment, they flew to Cleveland. At the airport Walker rented a Reliant and they drove up to Detroit, spending the night at the Dearborn Inn. Early the next morning, with a new rental car, a Buick Regal, they drove north to Grayling, four hours away in the pine flatlands of the state.

It was normal procedure, Walker tried to explain, all the fooling around with the route. The idea was to keep the competition off stride. "In case," he said, feeling foolish as he said it, "they're paying any attention."

"Sure," Karen said.

"In this business you're always looking over your shoulder."

"For the one who called?"

He had to think to remember whom she meant. "Among others," he said.

The town was clean and sun-drenched and thick with vacation traffic stopping off Interstate 75 to the Mackinac Bridge. At a real estate agency called Northwoods Homefinder, located in an A-frame made of peeled logs, Walker got the address of the summer lodge of Dorothy Cott Fairly but was told he'd never locate the place without help. He found a room in a Holiday Inn near a shopping development on the south edge of the town and suggested Karen wait for him there. The idea was it might be best if he approached the vice president alone, assuming he was at the woman's lodge. He'd interviewed him in the past but had had no contact with him since he left office. There was no telling how he'd react to a sudden visit. If it went well, if he agreed to an interview, Walker would ask about Karen's photographs.

"Sure," Karen said. She'd brought a bag of books and meant to catch up on her reading.

At an Amoco station Walker paid an attendant with a jeep done up in camouflage colors to lead him out to Mrs. Fairly's property. They took the North Down River Road from Grayling, then followed a twisting gravel road through heavy second-growth pine, the jeep ahead spewing out a cloud of dust. He was left on his own at an arched log gate, the gas station attendant pointing to the gate and then speeding on. There was no name or number, just a metal sign: PRIVATE. He drove in a mile or so on crushed stone before he saw the lodge, tucked away in pine and maple and white birch. It was long and low, made of nearly black logs and set on a slight rise of land. Walker left the Buick beside a dusty Cadillac parked in front of a four-stall garage made of the same dark logs. When he got close to the lodge, coming up the rise of land, he could hear the river in front and feel the coolness in the air.

The front of the lodge was all screened porch overlooking the river, dark beneath the trees. Upstream the river was fast, the surface cut with silver streaks in the sun where the water broke over rocks; in the front of the lodge it made a broad turn and slowed, the surface like oil. Downstream it widened again and the current quickened and then the river turned and disappeared into the trees. He watched it, hearing the sound, and then he noticed the other sound—the tap of a typewriter coming from the screened porch. The first thing he felt, standing there in the trees, was tired. A long trip, and made longer by the route. Then he felt foolish. Long, devious trips were nothing new; neither was not knowing what he was doing. But he'd thought that was behind him, the raw recruit marching to Harry Kane's orders; he'd thought that was over. A million dollars in the bank, you ought to have control over your life. But he was marching again and out on a river in the trees with a cover story no one ought to believe. Thinking about that, feeling foolish, he wondered if he remembered the route back to Grayling and the Holiday Inn near the shopping development and Karen.

Then he realized the typing had stopped. Except for that he might have left; he might have got back in the Buick and tried to find the way back. From the trees he looked into the screened porch across the front of the lodge. The vice president was standing there, looking out at him.

"I suppose I've been waiting for this," the vice president said. "I suppose I've been waiting for somebody to track me down."

In a corner of the porch a portable typewriter was placed on a card table. Beside the typewriter was a box of typing paper and on the other side a stack of typed pages about a half-inch high. There was a coffee mug on the table filled with yellow pencils and a pipe in a glass ashtray. The vice president was holding a mug of coffee.

"But I didn't expect you. I thought I was seeing a ghost out there." He'd motioned Walker onto the porch and into a padded wicker chair placed near the card table. His own chair was hard and bare. There was no other furniture on that part of the porch. "I thought it might be a summer intern from Traverse City or Mount Pleasant."

"Sorry to disappoint you."

"No. I didn't mean that." The vice president sat on his hard chair, the card table separating them. "I just can't believe it. Out of the blue like that."

"I wasn't sure you were here," Walker tried to explain. "I decided to take a chance."

"I'm here all right." Then the vice president became aware of the coffee mug he was holding and apologized for being a poor host. He left the porch, going back into the log house, and then came back with another mug. He was wearing house slippers, Walker noticed. They sipped the coffee for a while, studying each other. Then the vice president said, "You look about the same. Maybe a bit more prosperous."

"You too," Walker said. "You look well."

It was true. The vice president had gained weight but it was to his advantage. When he'd left office he'd been gaunt and haggard; now his cheeks were full and smooth. His black hair was combed straight back and neatly trimmed; at the temples were dabs of gray. He wore khaki trousers and a checked summer shirt, both carefully pressed. He was a handsome man who had always enhanced his appearance with fine clothing. In the past many had wondered why the president chose a running mate who made him appear drab and unappealing by comparison. Walker thought about that now. As far as physical appearance went, the vice president would have made a dazzling president.

Except for the carpet slippers and the pipe in the glass ashtray. They were out of character. They didn't fit. In the past he'd worn Italian shoes and smoked two-dollar cigars.

"I am," the vice president said. "I'm feeling fine."

"Good country air."

"Yes," the vice president said. "That might be it."

"Good for writing, too, I suppose."

"Do you think so?"

"Well," Walker said, "probably not for me. I've never been good at writing by myself, off somewhere. Could be why I'm a newspaperman."

When Walker lit a cigarette the vice president took a plastic pouch from his pocket and began filling the pipe. He didn't look comfortable doing it. He looked like he had to concentrate on what he was doing, keeping the tobacco from spilling, getting it down in the bowl, tamping it with his thumb and then tamping it some more. When he had the pipe going he said, "I'd enjoy talking with you about that. How you work." Then he leaned back in the chair, smiling. It was a smile Walker recognized. It was a smile the vice president used on reporters when he wanted to appear cooperative, when he wanted to appear open and ready to talk. It was a good smile. "But you didn't come for that."

"No," Walker said.

In power, first as governor and then as the president's running mate, the vice president had maintained a complex relationship with the press. In public he'd attacked the press at every opportunity, charging it with an Eastern liberal bias and with giving aid and comfort to the Soviets. Among media owners he'd been one of the most feared men in the land; they said he played shamelessly to the prejudices of the country. Privately, the vice president had got on well with working journalists, and until his final ordeal enjoyed a favorable press. He gave the impression of liking the company of journalists; whatever he said about their work, he implied, was at the behest of the president. They, in turn, to the irritation of editors and publishers, found themselves liking him. Watching him now, smoking a pipe he'd never smoked before, Walker understood the feeling. It was hard not to like the vice president. Alone across a table, he was a likable man.

"We get some newspapers out here," the vice president said.

"I'm clean on the California Connection."

"Not that," Walker said, and went into the series of profiles of former administration figures, the where-are-they-now things he was thinking about. He explained that what he was doing now was beginning spadework to see if the series had possibilities. It wasn't at all clear it had.

"You're the expert," the vice president said. "But it's not your sort of story, is it?"

Walker lit another cigarette to cover a sudden edge of nervousness and admitted it wasn't. Since the Potomac story he'd done only investigative reporting. The profiles, if he did them, would be a change of pace.

"Yes," the vice president said. "I can understand you might want that." Then he said, "At least everyone's out of jail now."

"That's what Sam Pearlman said."

"So that's how you found me."

"In part," Walker said.

"You know then I'm writing a book for him."

"A novel, he said."

The vice president looked down at the stack of pages beside the typewriter, smiling again, sheepishly now. "Maybe that's what it is."

"A political novel?"

"Murder mystery—set during a political campaign. Sam had something else in mind but I thought I might be able to handle this. The problem is I'm not sure who the killer is going to be." The vice president fussed with his pipe again, filling it, getting the smoke rising, using the pipe to think with the way he used to use cigars, rolling them around in his mouth. "You want to start the series with me. Is that the idea?"

"It's the way I'm thinking now."

The vice president looked beyond Walker, out at the green

woods pressed tightly around the lodge, thinking with the pipe. Then he leaned forward and said, "All right. But with an understanding. Everything is off the record for now. If you decide to go ahead with the story, come back and we'll see where we are."

"You want to see what I get from the others?"

"No. I don't care about the others. That's the last thing I care about." He smiled again, the sheepish smile. "Didn't Sam say something? I'm trying this book because I need the money."

Walker said Pearlman had brought it up.

"I'm not in a position to give anything away. I need to talk with Sam before we go on the record. And my friend here."

"Mrs. Fairly?"

"Yes," the vice president said. "Mrs. Fairly."

"I'm not sure how the paper would feel about it," Walker said. "It would have to be discussed."

"Shabby business," the vice president said, "checkbook journalism. It's just I don't have much to sell anymore."

Walker nodded.

"Agreed then?"

"Off the record," Walker said. "If it looks like the story will go, I'll get back to you."

"Fine," the vice president said, and leaned back in his hard chair. "More coffee?"

• 12 •

He seemed to hold nothing back. He said he was a step away from total failure. His wife had remarried and he seldom saw his children; he was in debt for old legal fees; his corporate friends, once vociferous defenders, wouldn't risk the bad publicity that would come from hiring him. For a while after he left office there were consulting jobs with Middle Eastern and African countries that brought him good fees, and there was the college lecture circuit; but after the Potomac affair there were other administration figures scrambling for a living and competition was stiff. The vice president's share of a rather specialized market had never been great. Now his share was zero.

What he had left was his benefactor, Mrs. Fairly. And Sam Pearlman. Pearlman thought a novel would reawaken public interest; if nothing else, it would show the vice president was still alive. Then could come his memoirs. Pearlman pointed out he was the only one of the old administration figures who hadn't written his; the president was on a fifth volume. The mystery novel had been his own idea. He got it when he read one of Margaret Truman's. He'd met her once and decided if she could do one anyone could. But he wasn't finding it easy. It was more work than he thought, and took more patience. Patience wasn't his strong suit; he'd been an action type, a doer. He wouldn't have gotten as far as he had without Mrs. Fairly. She'd given him the time and the place to work. He'd pledged to stay at the lodge until he finished at least a first draft.

When Walker brought up Mrs. Fairly's background the vice president was firm. He wanted her left out of the story; it would be a condition of his cooperation. She was a private person and wouldn't want her relationship with him to appear in print. For Walker's own information he would say they were recent acquaintances. They had met by accident at a dinner party given by former political acquaintances, and by accident found they had mutual needs—Mrs. Fairly for companionship during her summer at the lodge, the vice president for a living arrangement that let him work on his novel. When the vice president said companionship he looked closely at Walker, expecting a reaction; when there was none he went on. Mrs. Fairly was passionate about fly fishing, a sport she had learned from her father and pursued on the river since childhood; she had also taken an interest in his writing. In fact, she had become a stern taskmaster, insisting he spend every morning on the screened porch, writing. She didn't want him to leave the lodge for fear he would be distracted, nor did they have guests. Beside reading mysteries for help with his own, his only recreation was fishing.

"Really?" Walker said.

The vice president knew what he meant. In the past he'd preferred his recreation on golf courses and tennis courts, and not much of that. In the past his idea of an outing was a cocktail party on a board chairman's yacht or a winter week of parties at the better condominiums in Vail. But up here possibilities were limited. Up here there was fishing or nothing. So he was learning. He went out with Mrs. Fairly in the evenings and she was teaching him the mysteries of the fly rod. He was finding it like writing the novel. It took patience. When Walker asked if he was happy here, writing and fishing at a place in Michigan, the vice president said it wasn't a matter of being happy or unhappy. It was what there was. Having something was better than having nothing. But he admitted he wasn't looking forward to a winter here. Mrs. Fairly wanted him to stay if he hadn't finished the novel by then, and he was already thinking about that, wondering what it would be like when the snow came. It made him think about Palm Springs. He used to have a place there, if Walker remembered. But he had no complaints. He considered himself lucky to have Mrs. Fairly on his side. As far as he could tell no one else was.

When Walker asked about the past, about whether he thought much about that, the vice president said at one time he had. At one time the past had been all he thought about. But then he realized, since nothing could be changed, there was no point to it. The past was whatever it was. He wasn't expecting to be vindicated by history—the president was taking that position in regard to his own troubles, and the vice president wished him well. But he himself expected nothing from history. It could remember him as it wished. If he finished the novel and turned to his memoirs they would be a straightforward account of what had happened, the mistakes he'd made and the mistakes of others. He wouldn't use the memoirs to settle old scores or rewrite the record. They wouldn't be his version of the facts but, as far as possible, the facts themselves.

They saw Mrs. Fairly at the same time, coming up from the river and crossing the lawn to the lodge, walking briskly, water glistening on her waders. She wore a floppy green hat of a kind Walker recalled seeing in photos of jungle fighters in Vietnam and a green fishing vest bulging with fly boxes and hung with pieces of equipment. She loosely carried a fly rod, the tip pointing behind her. When she reached the porch she removed the jungle hat and vigorously shook her hair, short and steel-colored, smiling at the vice president and showing no surprise at the presence of a visitor.

"Join you in a few minutes," she said.

When she reappeared, entering the porch from the lodge, she wore khaki trousers with a wide Western belt and a checked shirt nearly the same as the vice president's. She was a small, weathered woman who made Walker think of Hemingway's widow. There was the same sharp-featured face, the same air of being a good sport. She didn't seem the vice president's type. In the past, even before the breakup of his marriage, he had been seen with tall, glossy women on his arm, women who only saw the sun when it was setting. Mrs. Fairly looked like an early-to-bed-early-to-rise woman; she looked as if a log lodge in the woods on a river was the place she belonged. It wasn't easy to think of her ever living in a place called Grosse Pointe Shores.

When the vice president introduced him she greeted Walker graciously. She said she'd recognized him at once. She remembered the photograph on the back of his book and then from television. The vice president had mentioned the possibility of a journalist learning of his whereabouts and wanting to do a story. But they hadn't expected a journalist from Washington. They hadn't expected him. "But how nice of you to visit us," Mrs. Fairly said, and reached out to the vice president, touching his hand. "Such a nice surprise."

The vice president got another wicker chair and then went back into the lodge and brought fresh mugs of coffee, padding about in his slippers. When he explained about the nature of Walker's visit, explaining carefully and leaving nothing out, Mrs. Fairly listened but said nothing. When he was finished she asked if Walker was a fisherman.

He admitted he wasn't.

"If you come back," the vice president said, "maybe you'd like to try it."

"You should," Mrs. Fairly said. "I'm afraid there isn't much to do otherwise." Again she reached out and touched the vice president's hand, her fingers lingering. "Except write of course."

Walker asked if she wrote herself.

"Oh, no." The thought seemed to amuse her. "I wouldn't know how to begin."

Walker turned the conversation to Mrs. Fairly's fishing. She said the river had once been famed for its rainbow trout but now, with more fishing pressure, there were more brown trout than rainbows and fewer large trout of any sort. Canoeists were also a plague, disturbing the natural habitat of the trout to say nothing of the serenity of the stream. The part of the river where the lodge was located was restricted to fly fishing and for that reason known locally as the "holy water"; but poachers came in at night, fishing with live bait, and killing, she feared, large numbers of trout. One fortunate thing was that the river near the lodge had deep holes that made wading difficult for the inexperienced. It was one of the few things that gave her hope for the river's future. Everything else—a litany of problems from acid rain to the introduction of more and more sand and silt into the river bed—pointed to decline.

When he finished his coffee Walker said he'd taken up enough of their time. For the moment he had all he needed from the vice president.

"But you have to stay for dinner," Mrs. Fairly said. "When you've come so far."

He had to explain then that a young woman, a friend from Washington, had accompanied him to Grayling. She was waiting for him at the Holiday Inn.

"Then you must go and get her," Mrs. Fairly said.

Then he had to explain that the young woman was a photographer. If the series of profiles he was planning went forward, she might do some photo work. Needless to say, she would do nothing without the vice president's consent.

"Don't be silly," Mrs. Fairly said. "She can take her pictures now."

"Of course," the vice president said.

"It's settled then." Mrs. Fairly touched the vice president's hand once again and said, "After dinner we're going fishing. There's a hatch of brown drakes at dusk we simply can't miss. You two can see us off."

The vice president mixed martinis on the screened porch and Karen took pictures of him in conversation with Walker. With their drinks in hand Mrs. Fairly guided them on a tour of the lodge, all north-woods rustic: stone fireplace, polished plank floors and heavy leather furniture, shotguns and rifles in a glass case, watercolor scenes of the river on the walls. Dinner was grilled venison, mixed vegetables, and a Mouton Cadet bordeaux. The vice president, affable and courtly, showered Karen with attention but left the conversation to Mrs. Fairly. The two women got on well together, Karen prompting Mrs. Fairly with questions about the woods and fishing and the lodge, and Mrs. Fairly treating her as if she were a younger daughter.

Coffee and brandy were on the porch, sitting in a semicircle of wicker chairs, watching the river grow darker and swallows skim the surface and the sun dip into the trees on the other side. When Mrs. Fairly said it was time for fishing, Walker and Karen walked with them to a log building behind the lodge that smelled of pine needles and was filled with canoes and fishing equipment and waders hanging from wooden pegs. The vice president had difficulty with his waders and Mrs. Fairly adjusted the suspender straps. Then she helped him into a fishing vest. Finally he put on a floppy green jungle hat like hers and she anointed it with Deep Woods mosquito spray, bending to her, his eyes closed against the mist.

Watching him then, Walker understood what had been in the back of his mind since Mrs. Fairly had come across the lawn from the river, walking briskly, her waders glistening. It was vague then, stronger when she touched the vice president's hand, letting her fingers linger. The touch had been possessive. Having something was better than having nothing, the vice president had said, and Mrs. Fairly was what he had. But there was a price to be paid. There was always a price to be paid. Standing there, bent to the mosquito spray, he was paying. Wearing waders and a bulging fishing vest; letting her dominate the dinner conversation; sitting at a card table on a hard chair in a corner of the porch trying to write a novel; maybe even padding around in carpet slippers: he was paying all the time. And it was probably only the tip of the iceberg. Walker knew he had no idea how much the vice president paid.

He understood too an odd bond he felt with the vice president. He wasn't at ease here, not in the rustic lodge of a woman who looked like Hemingway's widow on a river in the woods of Michigan, and neither was the vice president. The life they both gravitated to was politics and government and intrigues of power. They couldn't feel at ease removed from that. He wouldn't finish his novel here; in Washington he might, but not here. She would keep him at it until the snow came and turned the place into God knew what, and still he wouldn't finish it. He must wonder about leaving, putting a bad idea behind him, but where was he to go? Having something was better than having nothing. But not much, Walker decided. Not with the payments he had to make—the ones Walker knew about and the ones he didn't. The vice president was a politician and Walker never felt sorry for them. Nobody asked them to take up the life. But he felt sorry for the vice president now. A man paying like he was, you had to feel sorry.

"Got everything?" Mrs. Fairly asked him, and he checked off for her the contents of the vest: flashlight, fly boxes, scissors, leaders, glasses, tobacco. Then they were walking across the lawn to the river, Karen beside Mrs. Fairly, Walker with the vice president. "The hatch usually comes just before dark," she was telling Karen. "And we've been having a spinner fall after that—not the easiest time to fish, but the big trout become active."

Karen said, "I'd love to try it sometime."

"Well, you should, my dear. You'll just have to come back."

At the river Karen asked if she could take some pictures. They wouldn't be for Walker's article, if there was one; she wanted them to remember the evening. Mrs. Fairly stepped into the river, waiting for the vice president to come up beside her; they posed together, the water to the knees of their waders, smiling, jungle hats pushed back for the camera. Then Mrs. Fairly came back to the bank and kissed Karen on the cheek and shook Walker's hand. "Now do come see us again," she said. "Both of you." She moved out into the water, catching the current and turning to follow it downriver, stripping line from the reel. She flicked the fly rod back and forward and sent a quartering cast across the river, the cream-colored line flattening out over the water.

The vice president waited, letting her move ahead. Then he took a pipe out of the vest and began filling it. "Mosquito control," he said to Walker.

"No cigars?"

Shreds of tobacco fell from the bowl and drifted into the current. "Mrs. Fairly says her father thought the smell of mosquito lotion on the flies repelled the trout. He always smoked a pipe on the river." He lit the pipe and tossed the wooden match into the water. "It's a compromise with me. I use both."

"If I come back," Walker said, "I'll bring you cigars."

Karen took a picture of the vice president alone and then of he and Mrs. Fairly moving in single file down the river. When they turned into the trees she moved beside Walker. They listened to the river and watched night insects hovering over the shallows. Across the river the wall of trees was black now. Walker leaned down and dipped his hand in the water, feeling a sudden, hard cold. When he stood up, Karen raised her arms, encircling him, her eyes the only bright things in the darkness.

"I liked them both," she told him.

14

"Pearlman?"

"Steele?"

The morning light in the cocktail lounge of Cleveland-Hopkins International was faint and gray and the men moving through it had the manner of those who drink before noon.

They took chairs at distant tables, in low voices gave their orders to waitresses in abbreviated black skirts and fishnet stockings, examined the ceiling tile as they waited for drinks. Steele was on his second Bloody Mary when he saw Sam Pearlman at a far table.

"You here, too?"

"You see me? I must be here."

"So what's up?"

"Let's not shout across," Pearlman said. "Bring your drink over."

Steele's tie was askew and a single brass button held his plaid vest. Pearlman wore a denim leisure suit, badly wrinkled, and an open shirt with an oversized collar that flared out to his shoulders, showing a large medallion on a hairy chest.

"You don't look so hot, Bernie."

"I've seen you better, too."

Pearlman shrugged and poured a half shot of Jack Daniel's into a steaming cup of coffee.

"So what's up?" Steele asked again.

"Between planes from the coast. Atlanta I'm supposed to be."

"Yeah? I just came from there."

"Business?"

"Walker, that bastard."

Pearlman brightened. "What about him?"

"Nothing about him. I'm keeping an eye out is all."

"And?"

"You hearing, Sam? Nothing. I lost him—him and the girl. They take a plane to Atlanta, I lose them in the terminal. I walk twenty miles in the place."

"So why you're in Cleveland?"

"Where they came from Atlanta. By the time I figure it out

they're here and gone. They rent a car this time."

"You following him?"

"Hey, Sam. You put two and two together."

"On the Deep Well thing?"

Steele leaned back, thumbs hooked behind his vest. "He makes a mistake I'll nail his ass."

"You get the story you're a rich man. Remember our deal."

"Who's forgetting?"

"So keep at work."

"It's what I'm doing, Sam. It's why I'm here." Steele poked at the ice in his drink, chewed the celery, then leaned across the table, glaring at Pearlman through black-rimmed glasses. "But it's all crap. A wild goose chase."

Pearlman looked blank.

"He made it all up, Sam."

"No Deep Well?"

"Nothing."

"You sure?"

"I was sure I'd be dragging my ass around after him? I'm making sure."

Pearlman signaled a waitress for more coffee and tipped in the rest of his Jack Daniel's. "One thing I know. He ain't with Deep Well this trip."

Steele raised an eyebrow.

"He's seeing the vice president. The old one. Out in Michigan someplace."

"You sure?"

"He tells me as much. He's thinking of some profile things on the old administration guys. What they're doing now they're out of jail." Pearlman paused, reflecting over the rim of his cup. "He gets them talking it could sell."

"Who cares about the vice president," Steele mused.

Pearlman shrugged.

"Who cares about the old administration guys."

Pearlman shrugged again.

"It's a cover," Steele declared. "He's up to something else."

"The California Connection? A story to keep an eye on, too."

"What's the town, Sam?"

Pearlman thought, then recalled.

"Never heard of it."

"It's the place."

Steele was in line for Air Wisconsin to Detroit when he overheard the news.

He swung around on the couple behind him. *"What?"*

They began telling him they had heard it on the car radio on their way to the airport, coming in from Shaker Heights, but before they could finish he was sprinting down the corridor, thrusting people aside. From a pay phone he called his office and learned it was true. The wire services were carrying the story of the former vice president's death but the morning *Globe* had a by-lined account.

"Walker?"

"The lucky sonofabitch was right there," an editor told him.

Steele had the story read over the phone. It featured Walker nearly as much as the vice president. The reporter, in the small town of Grayling to do a profile of the vice president, had spoken with him during the afternoon and that evening had been a dinner guest at the fishing lodge of Mrs. Dorothy Cott

Fairly, the widow of a Detroit industrialist, where the vice president was spending the summer while writing a book. He had last seen the vice president when he and Mrs. Fairly left the lodge for some night fishing on a river called the Au Sable.

The vice president's body was discovered by Mrs. Fairly about midnight. During the night he had been fishing near her, but when she moved farther down the river she noticed after a while that he hadn't followed. She worked her way back up the stream and with a flashlight discovered the body face down in shallow water near the heavily wooded bank. She told authorities she believed he had stepped into a deep hole in the river, lost his balance, and been pulled under the surface when his waders filled with water. He wasn't, Mrs. Fairly said, an experienced fisherman nor was he as familiar as she with that part of the river. The Crawford County coroner confirmed that the vice president's death was due to drowning. The sheriff's office added that drowning deaths of fishermen on the river were rare though not unknown.

"They got pictures on page one," the editor told Steele. "The lucky sonofabitch had a free-lancer with him." Then he said, "What the hell you doing in Cleveland?"

"I had a premonition about him kicking off," Steele said. "I was on the way."

He got a chartered Cessna for a direct flight to Grayling. In the Crawford County courthouse he came in on a news conference in the sheriff's office. A *Chicago Tribune* reporter told him Walker had already filed a second story and then flown back to Washington; he'd left only crumbs behind. "Again," the reporter said.

On the sheriff's desk the photos taken by the free-lancer were displayed in a time sequence. There were pictures of Walker and the vice president with drinks in their hands and pictures of the vice president and his hostess in their fishing outfits. In all the pictures the vice president was smiling. There was a picture of him in the river, a pipe in his mouth and the water up to the knees of his waders, and then a picture of him following the woman down the river.

The sheriff, wearing a plaid shirt and string tie and green-tinted glasses under fluorescent lights, leaned on an edge of the desk, taking questions. He confirmed that the coroner had determined the vice president had been dead about an hour when Mrs. Fairly found him. There wasn't any sign on the body that he'd hit his head on a tree limb or fallen against a rock. Death was by drowning, plain and simple. It looked like he'd tried to get himself out of his waders, the waders that, filled with water, had pulled him under. His fishing vest was torn off and one of the wader suspenders was ripped from the metal fasteners that held it to the waders. It seemed there hadn't been time to get the other suspender off. If there had, he might have got the waders off. He might have been all right then.

"It's no easy thing," the sheriff said, "standing up in waders with a load of water in them and current coming down hard."

A reporter asked a question about fishing at that time of night.

"Nothing unusual about it," the sheriff said. "Do it myself. Sometimes fish the whole night. Depends on the fishing."

Another reporter asked if the vice president was a good fisherman.

"Must have been all right. Mrs. Fairly's real good."

Steele wanted to know about the relationship between Mrs. Fairly and the vice president.

"You'd better ask her about that," the sheriff said. "You can't ask him."

Where was she now?

"Back to her place down there in Grosse Point Shores."

What condition was she in?

The sheriff searched for the word he wanted. "Not so good. Depressed, you could say."

Did that mean she felt she was responsible for the accident?

"I wouldn't say that. But the fishing was her idea. And she was the one knew the river."

Steele asked about the photos of the vice president with a pipe in his mouth. He wasn't a pipe smoker.

"Must have become one."

Had there been any word from the vice president's former associates in the administration? Any official expression of condolence?

"Nope. Nothing like that."

Nothing from the former president?

"Nope."

How about the body? Were there arrangements?

"There doesn't seem much hurry about that. We're waiting to hear something from relatives."

"What relatives?" Steele pushed him.

"Well, just about anybody. Anybody wants to claim him."

16

The call came to Walker's desk at the *Globe*. "A half hour," Kane said. "Same number."

He got to the Capitol Hilton with a few minutes to spare. The pay phone with a view of the lobby, the one he'd used before, wasn't in use. A detail Kane had seen to? It was another thing he didn't want to think about. He stood by the phone and watched the clock without numbers above the registration desk, not thinking about it.

When Kane's call came there were the same background noises on the line, people talking and the low humming machine sound. Maybe it was the laundromat Kane said it was. It was the kind of place he would use. But Walker didn't want to think about that either.

Kane said. "So?"

"It's all in the story, Harry."

"Nothing else?"

"You tell me. It was your idea."

Kane said, "He have anything to say?"

"Not much. He was getting along as well as he could."

"What's that mean?"

"I don't know." Walker tried to remember how the vice president had looked on the screened porch when they talked, but what stayed in his mind was Karen's photo of him moving down the river behind Mrs. Fairly, the green jungle hat down over his face, the pipe in the corner of his mouth. "He was trying to fish and he didn't know how."

Kane waited for him to go on.

"He was writing a novel and didn't know how to do that either."

Kane waited some more and then said, "Sounds like he touched your heart."

"I felt sorry for him," Walker said. "He told me he was a step away from total failure."

Kane sounded surprised. "He said that? Very dramatic."

Walker looked out over the lobby. No convention types now. Just business types in summer suits and tall, thin women walking quickly toward the elevators. Washington types. In Washington there were always tall, thin women walking quickly. "Why did I go out there, Harry?"

"You talk about Deep Well?"

"Should we have?"

"He mention me?"

"No."

"Tell me about the woman."

"Small, determined. The outdoor type. She made me think of Hemingway's widow."

"Not exactly the old boy's type."

"No."

"You talk to her afterward?"

"She was gone by the time I heard. The sheriff's people up there got a statement from her."

"You see the body?"

"I identified it."

"They didn't ask her?"

"They wanted two IDs. No mistakes."

"And?"

"He hadn't been in the water long enough to make much difference. You couldn't tell. Except he'd scratched through to the skin trying to get the clothing off."

"The pictures in the paper. The girlfriend?"

"Look, Harry," Walker said. "I took her along and she happened to take some pictures. It's what she does. That's all there is to it."

"Except you didn't tell me."

"You didn't tell me why I went to see him."

"Okay," Kane said. "It's over now."

"Not quite."

"I'm grateful for the help," Kane said. "Leave it at that."

"No."

"You said something about an ordinary life."

"Up there," Walker said, "I felt sorry for him. He was hanging on by the fingertips. He was smoking a goddamn pipe because she thought it kept mosquitoes away. He was wearing house slippers because she probably thought that's what writers wear. Every night she took him out on that goddamn river and finally it killed him. I liked him, Harry, and I felt sorry for him and I want to know what I was doing up there."

"No you don't."

"Set it up, Harry."

Kane said, "That a threat?" He was silent, letting Walker hear the background voices, the humming machine sound. Then he said, "I'll be in touch."

"Good."

"I wouldn't be so sure," he said.

When Walker got back to the *Globe* there was another call, this one from Sam Pearlman.

"Long distance," Pearlman explained, "from Georgia. One of them minimum security places. Got a client here—white-collar crime, computer stuff. They tune in a company, take the dough, nobody even knows it's gone. He's blowing the whistle on the whole thing. Anyway I only got a minute."

Walker said, "It was all in the paper, Sam."

"Not all."

"No?"

"The book, I'm thinking about."

"He was working on it."

"Yeah, but what's on some paper? He got enough I could get a ghost, finish it up. One of them posthumous things. You know what I mean?"

"More or less."

"So you see some manuscript lying around?"

"You'd better ask the woman, Sam."

"She'd know?"

"If anyone."

"I get it," Pearlman said. "I'll be in touch. Maybe something better than the ghost. You saw him last. You're busted up. You want to do a little for the guy, so what you do, you finish up the book. A tribute thing. What do you think?"

"Not much."

"Don't pass it up too quick."

"I don't write fiction."

"Yeah?" Pearlman said. "It's not the way I hear it."

Dorothy Cott Fairly was waiting on another line. "I just wanted to say something," she said. "About the story."

Surprised by the call, Walker didn't respond at once.

"I know it must have been difficult. But it was—respectful, I suppose I want to say. I know he would have thought so." Mrs. Fairly paused, waiting for him. Then she said, "I just wanted to say that."

"I'm glad you liked it," he said finally.

"And the pictures," Mrs. Fairly said. "He looked so well in them. So happy really. Please tell Karen."

"I will," Walker said.

"The more I think about it, the more I realize how fortunate it was you both were there. Without you—without your story and the pictures—well, I don't know what it might have been like." She took a deep breath, as if forcing herself to continue, as if determined to finish what she had to say. "I must admit I was worried when I saw you there. I thought it might distract him from his work. It was so important that he find something—something he could do. But he was pleased to see you. I could tell that. And so pleased to have you and Karen for dinner—to have some guests."

"I'm glad," Walker said.

"But now I realize it was—well, a blessing really. I only wish we hadn't gone out fishing, that we had just spent the evening together. Just talking together. I'll never forgive myself for that."

"It wasn't your fault," Walker said.

"That's kind of you. But it was. I shouldn't have taken him to that part of the river. I shouldn't have left him alone. I shouldn't have gone out fishing at all with you and Karen there. It was," Mrs. Fairly said, "it was all my fault and I'll never forgive myself."

"Please," Walker said.

"No. I know what I did. I know I must face it." There was a deep breath again and after that silence on the line. Then Mrs. Fairly said, "But I didn't mean to say that. That isn't why I called. I just wanted to say how grateful I am that you and Karen were there—that you were the one who did the story. It's made it much easier."

"Good," Walker said.

"Your profiles," Mrs. Fairly said, and he could hear the effort in her voice to square her shoulders, to carry on. "Will you still be able to do them?"

"We'll see."

"I hope you can. And Karen her pictures."

"We'll have to see," he said again.

"I hope we meet again," Mrs. Fairly said. "Maybe we will."

"I hope so, too," Walker said.

"I just wanted to say something to you. I didn't want it to end so—abruptly."

"I'm glad you called."

"Thank you again," Mrs. Fairly said. "He would have wanted me to say that."

When Walker met her for lunch Karen said she didn't feel like eating, so they drove out Connecticut Avenue, left the car at the Shoreham Hotel, and spent the time walking in Rock

Creek Park. It was one of her favorite places in town. She said it was an antidote to the ponderous federal establishment and the ponderous types who worked in it. She said it was a place you could breathe without smelling car fumes and see some greenery that wasn't landscape design. For a while you could almost forget you were in Washington. If you could forget the heat and humidity you could almost believe you were in Michigan.

"I thought it was so lovely there," she said to Walker, her arm through his as they moved slowly along a cinder path, ignoring the noontime joggers.

"Not now?"

"How could I now? It seemed such a perfect place to write his novel and then it turned out so awful."

"You can't blame the place," he said. But he didn't believe that himself. The place was all wrong. If it hadn't been for the place the vice president would still be alive.

"I suppose," she said, and he could tell she didn't believe it either.

When he told her about the call from Mrs. Fairly, Karen said it was awful that she felt responsible for what had happened. She said she felt almost as bad for Mrs. Fairly as she did for the vice president. He was at peace but she would have to live with what had happened. She would never be able to escape it. That she had been pleased with Walker's story and Karen's pictures was at least something they had been able to do for her.

"It isn't much though, is it?"

"No," Walker said.

"And we won't see her again, will we?"

"No."

"Oh, God," Karen said.

They just walked then, their arms linked, following the

cinder path, not saying anything since there wasn't anything to say. Walker thought again about the place, about how cold the water had been to his touch, about the way the river below the lodge turned into the trees. Then he thought about how the vice president had looked in the waders and the way he bent to the mosquito spray and the way he filled his pipe and the sight of him on the porch in slippers. Nothing had been right. You added everything up, you couldn't have known he would die up there. But you knew he was out of his element and in trouble and hanging on by his fingertips.

"He never liked it up there," he said to Karen.

She stopped, looking at him with moist eyes. "But his writing and—"

"Not one goddamn bit."

"Oh, I hope you're wrong," she said.

Kane sent the signal through the *Times* and Walker took the usual precautions. But this time it was different. Kane was in his running outfit, bare legs stretched out on the cement of the parking garage, white socks to his knees, his back up against the low wall. But this time there was no Jameson and no plastic glasses. This time he didn't play the game. When Walker loosened his tie and slid down beside him Kane said, "You still want to know?"

Walker lit a cigarette, thinking there might be more, thinking Kane would drag out the preliminaries. But Kane said,

"The vice president didn't have an accident out there. He was murdered."

Walker just stared at him.

"It crossed your mind? You show up and he has a fatal accident. You think it was coincidence?" Kane looked away, out into the blue light of the parking garage, letting Walker stare at him. Then he said, "It never looks like murder, if it's what you're wondering."

"Murder, Harry?"

"They prefer as little fuss as possible. A plausible accident. A plausible illness. Based on your story my guess is she got him in a dangerous part of the river and waited for him to slip. Maybe nothing more than that. It hadn't worked, she would have tried something else. But the fishing accident was a nice touch. You there. The girlfriend taking pictures. Everybody smiling."

"Mrs. Fairly?"

"You think we're talking about someone else?" When Walker didn't respond Kane said, "Don't bother to check her background, by the way. Clean as a whistle."

After a while Walker told him about the phone call from Mrs. Fairly, about the way she had thanked him for the story and said the vice president would have been pleased.

"Maybe her first assignment," Kane said. "An organization the size of the repairmen, they nurse people along for years, use them for one thing."

"But why would she call me?"

"Tie up loose ends. Maybe she even had some feeling for the vice president. He wasn't a bad guy."

"Christ, Harry. *Murder?*"

Kane, watching Walker, didn't say anything. Then he said, "I don't suppose you know what a wading belt is. It's a belt fishermen wear outside waders when they're in tricky water. If they fall the belt keeps the waders from filling with water. At least that's the idea. The vice president wasn't wearing one."

"How do you know that?"

"The girlfriend's pictures. A little something Mrs. Fairly hadn't told him about."

"She had one on?"

"A mistake," Kane said. "She wanted the pictures for the record but she forgot about the wading belt. That was her first assignment; it's also her last."

"What?"

"That line of work, the rules are a bit more stringent than you're used to. No mistakes."

Walker asked about the sheriff.

"He noticed when he saw the pictures. Then he checked her waders back at her lodge. An Orvis belt. Quality stuff. But he was persuaded not to raise the matter with Mrs. Fairly."

"But if she killed him."

"There was no proof of anything," Kane said. "Just a little mistake she made."

Walker was silent, smoking another cigarette, wishing Kane had brought the Jameson again, wishing even they were back at the dump of a truck stop in Sutland and he could order a drink from the sleepy waitress. With a drink he might be able to think. Without one his mind took in what Kane said but didn't do anything with it; what he said was there, what he'd told Kane he wanted to know about the vice president, but he couldn't see the next step. He knew there was one but he couldn't see where it was. Then Kane pointed it out.

"Did the old boy notice? You're wondering about that?"

"Yes," Walker said.

"He might have noticed she had a wading belt and he didn't. Maybe it was always that way, maybe just that night. If it was that night and he noticed then he made a bad mistake. He should have stuck to you like glue. You were his ticket out of there alive. On the other hand, maybe he thought he could handle it. He always liked a tough situation. Or maybe he never noticed anything different. Maybe he thought belts were for women. In that case he never had an idea what hit him."

"The book he was doing," Walker said. "It was a murder mystery."

"So you think that's significant?"

"I don't know."

"Neither do I," Kane said.

Walker rubbed out his cigarette on the concrete and lit another. He could feel Kane watching him in the flare of the match, seeing his hands shake. It wasn't anything Kane had said. It was another step to take; he could see it now. Even without a drink he could see this one.

"Enough?" Kane asked him.

"No."

"Ask then."

"You know."

"It's your party," Kane said.

"What did he have to do with it, Harry?"

"Thought you'd never ask," Kane said.

"How much do you know about my White House job?" Kane asked him.

"That you were probably a company plant," Walker said.

"Good," Kane said. "I thought you knew that. We can start there."

But first he had to go back, giving the background. His job with the company, back then, was what might be called an in-house spook. One of the complications of the spying business is you need people keeping an eye on the spies. The whole point about spies is they can't be trusted. So that was Kane's job, back then; he kept an eye on the spies. Someone was keeping an eye on him, too, though he never knew about it. His cover was that he was coordinator of internal communications in the operations section—to all appearances a minor staff functionary. He made sure memos flowed properly and were properly filed or destroyed. No one paid much attention to him, which of course was the point. But the real job all along was company spook in operations, reporting to the head of the section.

When the new administration came in they wanted an inhouse spook for the White House. They didn't trust any of their own people—for good reason it turned out. So they came to the company for help and the director suggested Kane. He told them Kane was near retirement. The agreement was Kane would leave the company and work the rest of the time for the president's people, reporting to them. They were probably smart enough to know he'd still be working for the company, but they were willing to go along with that to get an experienced person. Maybe they were smart enough to know the company would have someone in the White House anyway, since it always had, and this way they would maybe know who. Maybe that was the reason they came to the company in the first place. The president's people were like that. They thought they had everything figured out.

So Kane had two jobs and the same cover. He was a guy near retirement with an office in the White House basement who coordinated the memos. Of course the president's people were playing over their heads. They usually were. They had the fatal weakness of underestimating everyone except themselves. They wanted nickle-and-dime things from Kane—who in the place was sleeping around or drinking himself to death or talking to reporters like Walker. They thought they needed that sort of thing to keep people in line. And they thought they had him boxed in to that sort of thing. If he got into anything deeper they could scream the company had put a plant in the White House and Kane's ass would be on the line. The company would deny it and he'd have to handle it himself. But he got into something deeper anyway.

That was where the vice president came in.

You had to remember how clean he looked at one time. You had to remember that when the Potomac stuff started coming out he was the only one in the administration who wasn't touched. They had him locked out of all the important things, so he knew nothing about it. That began to burn some of the president's people, the vice president looking like Mr. Clean when the trouble began to come in. It looked to them like all he had to do was keep his distance and the party would hand him the next nomination. Their ship was going down, his was coming in. So they started leaking the things about his financial dealings. That's how they operated. They screwed anyone in sight. Their own people, the other side—it didn't matter. Hardball, they called it.

It didn't take the vice president long to figure it was coming from them and he decided to fight back. You had to remember how he loved a fight, what a tough guy he could be. He decided to put some fuel on the Potomac stuff. Maybe he was thinking the diversion would help him ride out his own problems, or maybe he thought he was shooting for the presidency. Anyway, he came to Kane for help. That he picked Kane was an odd piece of luck. Or maybe it wasn't luck. Maybe the vice president had a hunch. Anyway, he needed someone in the White House he could see on a casual basis without raising suspicions, and someone who wasn't in the inner circle. He was right on the first point, wrong on the second. But he didn't know that; all he knew was Kane was a guy who worked in the White House basement, filing paper. Now and then he'd stop by Kane's office and talk. Now and then they had a drink together. You had to remember he had nothing to do; he spent his days walking around the White House and the Senate, talking to people. At the same time, Kane was cultivating him, since the vice president was one of the people he was supposed to be keeping an eye on. When he thought he had Kane on his side, Kane agreeing with what his business friends were saying about his troubles, he asked him to leak some Potomac stuff to the press. He didn't want to know how Kane did it. He wanted deniability. He probably didn't know how Kane did it until he read Walker and Bickel's book. He told Kane he was leaking the Potomac stuff for patriotic reasons, for the good of the country, and maybe there was something to that. But the real reason was he wanted to get even with the president's people. They screwed him, he screwed them back. That's how it was in the White House then.

Now go back a step. Remember the president's people kept the vice president in the dark about what was going on, so he had to get the Potomac stuff elsewhere. He didn't have anything on his own. Keep that in mind. But it didn't matter where the stuff was coming from because Kane already had it; everything the vice president passed him he already had. It was his business to have that stuff and he had it. Of course Kane could have turned in the vice-president to the president's people, and the vice president must have known that was a possibility. But he had to chance it. His back was against the wall by then. The strange thing was, going to Kane, he made the perfect choice. He chose the one guy in the White House he could trust. Maybe it was dumb luck, maybe something else. Maybe it was instinct. If it was instinct then he might have made a halfway decent president.

So Kane began passing on to Walker what the vice president told him and what he knew himself. He wasn't operating on his own. You had to remember the time. The White House had put up the barricades; the people in there were so busy fighting the Potomac stuff the work of the place was at a standstill. If the Soviets were going to move, it was the time; even if they weren't, it wasn't clear anymore whose hand was on the button, or to what purpose. The risk was too big. So the company made a judgment: Let it come out. Get the administration out and a new one in before it's too late. That was when Walker began getting the signals in his morning *Times*.

"So the vice president was murdered because the repairmen knew he'd been the real Deep Well."

"Yes," Kane said.

"Why didn't they know before?"

"They didn't think he had the information. They thought they had him closed out."

"And they never suspected you?"

"They had no reason. As far as they knew, I had nothing. There were dozens of people like me in the place. Only the president's top people knew my real job and they thought they had me as closed out as the vice president."

"And they know now?"

"Not them. Those guys write books for your friend Pearlman. They still don't know what hit them."

"The repairmen then."

"They figured out about the vice president. It was a process of elimination. It had to be someone and they found who."

"And now they know about you, too."

"They know the vice president didn't pass the stuff to you himself. So there must have been another leak beyond him. They know that."

"But do they know it's you, Harry?"

Kane said, "Now you know what I know. Satisfied?"

* * *

He left the parking garage the usual way, going first, Kane staying behind. But when he got to the end of the ramp he turned and came back, coming up through the blue light into the gloom. Kane hadn't moved from the concrete floor.

"One thing, Harry."

Kane was looking at him.

"You didn't bring a bottle."

Kane shrugged. "It was your party."

"It wasn't the first time," Walker said.

"It was the first time it started with a threat."

"I felt sorry for him, Harry. He was in bad shape up there. You had to see him, the situation he was in. He had no alternatives. That was the reason."

Walker waited, looking down at him, and finally Kane said, "So you said before. He touched your tender little heart."

"He shouldn't have?"

"Your line of work," Kane said, "what's it matter." Then he said, "Okay. Next time I bring the bottle."

"What next time?"

"There'll be one," Kane said.

18

Like most good ideas this one came to the agent in a flash of inspiration.

A book saying there was no Deep Well and never had been could sell as well as one saying who the guy was. All this time, trying to track him down, get the guy's name, he'd been missing something nearly as good. Conspiracy books were hot items—the Kennedys, King, big oil, a hit on the pope, it didn't matter what as long as you showed there was dirty business involved. Sam Pearlman didn't know if the Deep Well thing qualified as a conspiracy, but if there was no Deep Well there was plenty of dirty business.

He could see himself promoting it. "Look, I handled this book of Walker's because I believed in it. It was a very significant story. History. Now I learn there was shit involved. So I want to see the right story get out, clear up my own conscience. You know what I mean?"

Back in Washington the first thing Pearlman did was arrange a lunch with Steele at Sans Souci. It wasn't the sort of place he ordinarily took him. For a guy who wore a plaid vest the year around and bought cigars five for a buck Blackie's House of Beef was a better spot. But he wanted an environment in which he felt himself most persuasive. You could figure on Buchwald being at Sans Souci, maybe Kissinger if he was in town, Tom Wicker, Herman Wouk, Teddy White, successful types whose presence helped his clients grasp the opportunities Pearlman spread before them. He got a decent table and waited until the second martini before turning the conversation to business.

"So you got nothing in Michigan, Bernie."

Steele, morose, a flowered tie hanging outside his vest like a limp flag, said, "Crumbs. It's all the bastard left."

"Walker, you mean?"

"Who else."

With his little finger Pearlman stirred the ice in his drink. "You happen to see any manuscript up there?"

Steele stared over Pearlman's shoulder, taking no interest in the surroundings or the question.

"The guy was doing a novel for me," Pearlman explained. "Walker said he saw him working on it. But I can't find out nothing. The woman he was with is nowhere. It's why I asked."

"You try the sheriff?" Steele offered.

"He said there was nothing left but the guy's clothes."

"Then maybe there wasn't any novel," Steele said. "Walker's winged it before."

"Yeah," Pearlman said, and finished off the martini. He removed his glasses and polished them with a monogrammed handkerchief, concentrating now. "It's what I wanted to talk about."

Over lunch of rockfish with sorrel and a California white he outlined his idea, trying to develop some enthusiasm. "I been thinking about it every minute since you told me in Cleveland. No Deep Well. A book saying it would sell like a sonofabitch. All the people bought the other book have to buy this, see how they got it wrong. They make a new movie clear up the other one. The point is, you got an audience before you start."

Steele shrugged, showing no interest.

"A book like that," Pearlman said, "you also got Walker squirming."

Steele's eyes shifted then, focusing on him.

"How'd the president's guys say? He'd be twisting on some rope."

"Dangling by the balls," Steele said.

"Anyway you want it." Pearlman paused, his fork raised. "You can do the book it is."

"I can do it."

"Sure you can. But you got the facts cold?"

"Cold enough."

Pearlman asked for a little explanation. Just so he'd have a better grip on the thing.

Steele thought a moment, then leaned across the table, tie trailing across the plate but a gleam in his eye. "Say I do a book ticking off all the people it could have been but wasn't. I got denials plus other stuff to show it couldn't have been them. I go through the list, everybody anybody ever heard of."

"I got some names, too," Pearlman broke in. "I'll pass them on."

"So I go through the list, one name after another. Very logical. And it adds up to zero. No Deep Well."

"Logical is good," Pearlman said. "Gives it a tone."

"So then I draw the conclusion. There never was a Deep Well. Walker made it all up to cover his lousy ass."

Pearlman chewed reflectively. "Sounds okay," he said finally. "But one question. What happens Walker sticks to his story?"

Steele almost smiled. "The beauty of it, Sam. He can't refute the conclusion unless he produces Deep Well."

"So he says you got it wrong."

"But he can't *prove* it, Sam. My word against his and I got the logic."

"You maybe got a point," Pearlman mused.

Steele lit a White Owl and leaned back in the chair, his case made.

"And he produces the guy," Pearlman went on, "we say our book did it. Made him go public."

"He's got nothing to go public with."

"In case, Bernie. Something like this, you figure all the sides."

· 19 ·

The official memorial service for the vice president in the Senate chamber over which he had once presided was short and dispirited. There were more secretaries and staff people in attendance than congressmen and administration officials, and those who had come seemed faintly embarrassed and anxious to leave. There were no family members and none of the vice president's former friends from business and entertainment. The funeral service had been held the day before in Palm Springs, where the vice president once had his home; after that the body was cremated and the ashes sprinkled in the desert. The wire story had received only a few lines in the *Globe*. It said a handful of mourners had turned out, reminding Walker of the funeral of Gatsby in Fitzgerald's novel. The poor sonofabitch, he'd thought.

He dimly listened now to the Senate chaplain speak of the toll exacted from body and soul by government service. Around him people sat with their heads down, inspecting their fingernails. After it was over he smoked a cigarette on the Capitol steps, the day overcast and humid, looking down over the mall toward the Washington Monument. It was the sort of day that made you wonder why they put the town in a Southern swamp, made you wonder what a hellhole it must have been before air conditioning. He took off his suit coat and folded it over his arm. It wasn't the weather that was on his mind; it was his feeling for the vice president, a feeling he couldn't shake. That nobody cared made it worse. The vice president had been a heartbeat away from every politician's furtive dream, yet ended up with nothing. The scandal that had overtaken him in the White House had destroyed his career, and his death had been unusually cruel. He'd been murdered, Kane said, and nothing would be done about it. Even the fact of the murder, bringing the vice president whatever sympathy it would, softening the public memory if it would, had to remain hidden. Kane knew and the company knew and now Walker knew; but nothing would be done. The best stories in town always went unwritten. He'd once feared that would happen with the Potomac affair; then Kane stepped in. This time was different; this time Kane wouldn't lift a finger. With his shoe Walker ground the cigarette against the Capitol's marble steps, a poor act of revenge in the vice president's name.

Cruel.

In the middle of the night he sat up in Karen's bed, rubbing his eyes, trying to hold the thought that had come to him. Beside him Karen shifted under the sheet, moving toward him, coming up from sleep, too. The vice president's death *had* been cruel. But it wasn't only the manner of his dying or Mrs. Fairly's part in it or the machinations of the repairmen. It wasn't the funeral no one attended or the memorial service no one cared about or the silence that was over it all and would stay that way. It was Harry Kane. However it happened up there in the woods, Kane was responsible for the vice president's death. He had caused it to happen as surely as if he'd led the vice president into dangerous water himself, and he'd used Walker as his emissary. That hadn't been clear to him before but it was now. He hadn't seen it before but he did now. Harry Kane was responsible for the vice president's death.

"What is it?" Karen asked him.

"Nothing." Then he said, "I just realized something I should have realized before."

She pushed herself up in the bed and touched his cheek. "Can I help?"

"I'm afraid not."

"I will, you know."

Walker took her hand, holding it. "I'm sorry I woke you."

"Can you go back to sleep?"

"Sure."

But he couldn't. He stared into the darkness, waiting for morning. He owed Kane something; he owed him almost everything. But he didn't owe him complicity in a murder. He hadn't known that's what it was; he'd gone up there because Kane had asked him to and because he owed Kane something. He had no way of knowing it might happen. But Kane had. That was the point of Kane sending him up there: Kane had known it might. It was his way of finding out. Because it had, he didn't owe Kane anything anymore. He'd paid Kane back; he'd even done more than that. He'd done all the paying he was going to do. It was Kane's turn now.

He made the call from Karen's apartment while she was still asleep. Before he left he wrote a note, saying he'd explain later, and placed it on the kitchen counter. He took breakfast earlier than usual at Sholl's Colonial, tea and an English muffin, keeping an eye on his watch and the delicatessen across the street. Shortly before nine he left and drove out to some public tennis courts in Silver Springs, following the sketchy directions he'd been given. He kept watching the rearview mirror, but there was nothing to see.

Kane was there, lobbing the ball back and forth with a thin blonde with a deep tan and firm, athletic legs. The girl wasn't especially pretty but she could play tennis. She had Kane trotting back and forth across the court. Watching from the Mercedes parked in the cinder lot, Walker decided the girl could pass as Kane's granddaughter. He remained in the parking lot, waiting, but no one else pulled in.

Finally he got out of the car and walked to the chain-link fence around the court where Kane and the girl were playing, not in a hurry now that he was here and no one had followed him. He watched them play for several minutes. When Kane came to the fence to retrieve the ball he finally noticed him. He picked up the ball and met Walker's eye. But he didn't say anything; he went on with the game, playing better Walker thought, talking with the girl across the net, joking with her, giving no sign of recognition. Walker didn't move. He lit a cigarette and leaned against the fence, watching the game.

When it was over Kane talked with the girl at the net. "Sure, Harry," Walker heard her say. Then she rose to her toes and leaned across the net, kissing him on the lips. The girl came around the net and Kane walked with her across the cinder lot to a dusty Toyota parked in the shade. Before the girl got into the car she kissed Kane again, leaning into him. Kane waved as the girl drove out of the lot.

When he came back to the court Walker said, "Yours?"

"Martha or the car?"

"So that's Martha."

"The car's hers," Kane said. He didn't look at Walker. He put the tennis balls they had been using into a can and put the can into a nylon athletic bag; then he put his racket inside the bag, the handle angled out the zippered opening. When Kane left the court two teenage boys entered it and began slamming an orange ball back and forth. On wood benches near the other courts other players waited, all young, rackets leaning against tanned legs. Beyond the courts, across the brown grass of a small park, a pickup basketball game was underway on an asphalt court. There were no nets on the baskets. A man wearing a Panama hat against the sun and with a cocker spaniel on a leash had stopped to watch. No one in the park was paying any attention to the thin older man in a white tennis outfit and the younger man in a tan summer suit.

From the court Kane walked slowly to a water fountain, Walker following. Then they walked slowly across the parking lot to the shade where the girl's Toyota had been parked. Kane stopped there and looked back at the small park, inspecting it. In daylight his face was more lined than it had seemed in the parking garage and the dump of a truck stop; there were deep creases around the mouth and at the edges of the eyes. Stress lines. Exercise lines. He was serious about his health. That seemed strange for someone in Kane's line of work. You didn't expect those people to worry about the same things that worried everybody else. You didn't expect them to die of the same ailments that overtook everyone else. Then Kane was looking at Walker.

"You want to explain?"

"It took me a while," Walker said. "It shouldn't have but it did. I was thinking more about him than you. It took me a while to realize you sacrificed that poor sonofabitch to find out how close the repairmen were to you."

"You know what you're doing coming here?"

"I think so," Walker said.

"You're risking my neck."

"Then I know."

"And the point is?"

"The way you risked his," Walker said. "That's the point."

"That's all?"

"And the rest of the story."

"To salve your conscience?"

"No," Walker said. "Just to know. Just to know why you let him die like that."

"You won't feel any better."

"I know that."

"And our little relationship," Kane said. "You've finished that."

"I know that, too."

"You think you know a lot."

"No."

"You're right about that."

20

They needed Walker's car, Kane said. They needed to take a drive first. Now that Walker had forced his hand, Kane said he had to move sooner than he'd planned. It wasn't unexpected, what he had to do; it was just more urgent. That meant it had to be done now.

Kane drove. He turned the Mercedes out of the parking lot onto the suburban street; in a few minutes they were on the Capital Beltway, heading toward Bethesda. Then Kane turned off and they were heading back to town on Highway 185. After that they were on a suburban street again, passing large homes with screened porches and then the homes grew smaller and were closer together and the maintenance dropped off and then they were in a suburban slum. When they came to a mobile home park in the suburban slum Kane pulled the car to the curb.

"We need an understanding," he said, and looked at Walker, the exercise lines tight around his mouth. "You want to know, you'll know. This is what you want to know."

A sign at the entrance to the mobile home park, faded green letters stenciled on a piece of cracked plywood, said FOREST ESTATES. Walker looked but couldn't see a tree in the place. Sun baked the aluminum boxes, heat waves shimmering over the roofs.

"I tell you what to do," Kane said, "do it. No questions." Then he said, "It's like the vice president up there. No margin for error."

"He didn't know what was happening," Walker said. "You do."

"He should have known," Kane said.

Kane turned the car into Forest Estates and followed a curving asphalt street, driving carefully, watching out for children playing on the edge of the street. On a cul-de-sac he stopped the car behind the dusty Toyota. It was parked in front of a mobile home, two-tone beige with black metal steps leading to the door, a mobile home that looked like every other mobile home in the place. "Home sweet home," he said to Walker. Then he took the athletic bag from the seat and said, "We go in, stay behind me."

Before they reached it the screen door of the mobile home swung open and Martha, the thin blonde with the tanned legs, was standing there, waiting for them. She looked at Kane and then her eye shifted and she took in Walker over his shoulder, just glancing at him.

"Waiting?" Kane said.

He stood on the metal steps until she moved back inside the

mobile home, then he came in and stood facing her. She was still dressed in her tennis shorts, blond hair still pressed against a moist forehead. Her tennis racket had been tossed onto a davenport pushed back against a paneled wall. "I heard the car," she said, and smiled, looking only at Kane now.

"You don't remember," Kane said, "he's the one you saw."

Her legs were spread, hands on hard, straight hips. She kept her eyes on Kane.

"His car," Kane said. "The fruit of past labors."

"Nice," Martha said.

"Glad you like it," Kane said. "You won't mind a ride."

"Now, Harry?"

"Any reason why not?"

She began backing away from him then, moving casually, easily, not turning away but putting space between them. Kane let her reach the kitchen. Behind her was a narrow hallway with a closed door at the end. "No," he said.

For a moment she looked away from him, down at her shorts and tanned legs and white sneakers. "It won't take a sec."

"No."

Kane slid open the zipper of the athletic bag and reached inside with his free hand. The gun was small and dull black and had a flat, squared-off barrel. He extended his arm, leveling it at her. Behind him Walker took a step forward and then stopped, watching the girl's face. There was no expression on it. She was looking into Kane's eyes, gauging him.

Kane said, "It won't make a sound."

Martha kept her eyes on him. Then she said, "Where?"

"Where someone else deals with you. Here I do."

Walker drove, Kane and the girl in the back seat. Kane said to take the Beltway east and then south past Goddard Space Flight Center and Andrews Air Force Base. He said to drive with the flow of traffic. In the mobile home he'd taken the can of tennis balls and the racket out of the athletic bag, then put his hand in with the gun, holding the bag from the straps with his other hand. They came out of the mobile home that way, Kane holding the gun in the athletic bag and the girl walking in front of him. Walker held the door open while they got in the back seat. He looked in the rearview mirror now but he couldn't see the bag. He could only see Kane and the girl, looking back at him.

At one point Kane said to her, "I've got some books for you. I've been meaning to tell you. Potomac books. You'll have time to read." The girl didn't say anything and Kane said nothing more.

When they had crossed the Potomac and were in Virginia Kane said to take Interstate 95 south to the Triangle exit near the Marine Corps Reservation. After that there were several turns and then they were on a narrow asphalt road winding through thick woods; now and then there was a mailbox on the road and a house set back in the trees. Kane told Walker to slow down, then to turn off the road at one of the mailboxes. The house at the end of a crushed-stone driveway was a redbrick ranch with a fussy lawn and crepe myrtles in bloom and beds of impatiens and bird feeders near the windows. It could have been the home of a retired military man and his wife. It could have been the home of anyone.

When Walker looked in the mirror Kane nodded to him. He got out and opened the door on the girl's side. He could see the athletic bag then, resting on Kane's lap, his hand still inside. Kane followed the girl across a flagstone walk to a side door of the house, holding the bag now with his other hand. When they reached the door it was opened from inside, a woman's bare arm holding it open, and Kane and the girl went inside. Walker, waiting in the sun beside the car, lit a cigarette then.

He was half done with it when Kane came out of the house. He didn't have the athletic bag now. He came back down the flagstone walk in his tennis outfit and said to Walker, "Care for some breakfast?"

"You said there would be another time," Walker said. "This was what you meant? You knew I'd come to the tennis court. You knew it was the only place I could find you. You must have known or you wouldn't have brought a gun. Or was there always a gun? Was there always one in the backpack?"

"No," Kane said.

"You brought it this time because you knew I'd come out there and Martha would see me."

Kane looked at him. "It wasn't what you wanted?"

"I wanted to put some heat on you, Harry. I wanted to put heat on you for what you did to him."

"You said that before."

"You knew I would. That's why you were ready."

Kane was still looking at him, the exercise lines still tight and deep around his mouth. "What I know is you. I knew you wouldn't forget about him. You didn't know enough to forget. You'd have to get even with me and the only way you could do it was to go public. That's what I knew."

The booth they were in at an Exxon truck plaza on Interstate 95, headed back to town, had a view of rows of pumps under a metal canopy and diesels stacked up on the edge of the parking area. Kane had told the hostess they wanted a booth at a window. When Walker asked if that meant they had been followed, Kane said it was possible since anything was possible. But it wasn't likely. The likely thing was Martha was on her own. If it went wrong, the way it just had, the repairmen would cut their losses with her; they wouldn't want anyone else involved. Nonetheless, Kane kept an eye on the parking area while they ate, trucker's special for him—eggs, sausage, wheat cakes, toast—only tea for Walker. It was a sizeable group, he reminded Walker. Better to believe what could happen is happening. That way you kept functioning. That was why he'd brought the gun to the tennis courts, knowing everything. There would be no time left then.

"You knew me," Walker said. "You knew her, too."

"I knew enough. Sweet young thing like that, she moves in with me. It's when I got the gun."

"That's when you knew about the repairmen?"

"It occurred to me. Then your friend Pearlman showed up."

"You thought she would kill you, Harry?"

Kane shrugged. "The one you're worked up about," he said. "He got Mrs. Fairly. I got Martha."

"You thought if you went back there after she saw me—you thought she'd kill you then?"

"The way it worked before," Kane said.

Walker lit a cigarette then, pulling the smoke in hard, thinking with it. After a while, not expecting the answer, he asked Kane anyway. "Where did we take her, Harry?"

"A place."

"Company place?"

"You worry about this, too," Kane said. "How come you never worried about running the old administration out?"

"I did."

"You worried until you sat down at the typewriter," Kane said. "Then you stopped." When Walker didn't say anything Kane said, "They keep Martha out of trouble a while. It's all they do. Swear to God."

It wasn't his usual breakfast, Kane explained on the drive back to town, taking the same route, following the Beltway around to the east. It was because he might not have a regular meal for a while. It was because he would be traveling again and there were things to see to before that.

Kane said to drive to Forest Estates. He had things to settle there and he wanted to get some clothes on. He said it was okay to go back there now; there would be people watching the place now. When they got there Walker would drop him off and that would be the end of it. "What you said you want to find out," he said. "You better find out now."

But he didn't wait for the questions. What he'd needed, he explained, was to determine how close the repairmen were. He'd acquired Martha and the vice president was up there on a river with Mrs. Fairly. And then Sam Pearlman showed up at Forest Estates. It was suggestive, you could say. But he needed more than that. So he met with Pearlman and sent Walker up there, seeing what the reaction would be. Pearlman was a dead end. The other, so to speak, wasn't. Walker and the vice president, meeting like that, it was all they needed; it satisfied their idea of what fit together.

"It could have been what I said," Walker said. "It could have been a profile."

But not to them. It was what they decided it was, Walker and the vice president together again. You had to remember they were tired of waiting. You had to remember they always had a rough sense of justice. It turned out they made a mistake about the vice president, it wasn't the sort of thing to bother them. You hang an innocent murderer now and then, you don't stop hanging the rest. That was the kind of chickenshit country the repairmen meant to fix.

"Did he know it?" Walker asked. "When I was there, did he know what it meant?"

If he didn't he should have. The vice president knew from the start the game he was playing. He knew those guys. He was there when they were in their prime. He knew what it meant to help bring down an administration when it was their job to keep it going. He knew they wouldn't forget something like that. Whether he knew what might happen when Walker showed up depended on whether he guessed about Mrs. Fairly. If he thought she was good fortune dropped in his lap then he didn't know what it meant. On the other hand nobody ever said he was dumb. They said he was a crook.

"It doesn't change anything," Walker said. "You sacrificed him, Harry. And you used me to do it."

He'd used Walker to find out how close the repairmen were. If they had figured out about the vice president then they were a step closer than they had been. If they knew about the vice president they also knew he wasn't the one who passed the stuff to Walker and Bickel. It had to have come from someone else and they still hadn't figured out who it was. Walker showing up at the tennis courts with Kane, then they knew about that, too. They knew all they needed to know. As for Kane sacrificing the vice president to save his own precious ass, he wouldn't argue the point. People were sacrificed all the time and for lots of reasons. He remembered an administration sacrificed for stories in a goddamn newspaper.

* * *

Walker said to Kane, "You said you weren't worried Sam Pearlman found your place. You said you knew why. It was Martha that told him."

"Very likely."

"But you asked me if I knew how Pearlman found you. You already knew how."

"Double-checking," Kane said. "A weakness I have." Then he said, "They were getting anxious so they had Martha get in touch with Pearlman. We waited longer, you might have heard from Mrs. Fairly. She might have asked you up there to do a story about the vice president. Something like that. We waited for that, I wouldn't have blood on my hands."

After a while, moving west now on the Beltway above the town, Walker said, "You hadn't come back in the first place none of it would have happened."

"You think so?"

"Why then?"

"You want to know," Kane said, "you'll know."

Steele was at his desk at the *Times*, vest unbuttoned, unlit White Owl thrust toward a video terminal, when a call came through from Sam Pearlman.

"What's up, Bernie?"

"You're the one called," Steele said. "What's up yourself?"

"Something on my mind," Pearlman told him. "I had to check."

"So check."

"You know a guy named Kane? First name Harry. He was in the White House with those other guys. Did something with the memos."

"So?"

"You know him, I'm asking."

"A guy I checked," Steele said. "He was down the basement somewhere. A nobody."

"I checked him, too. One day we played some tennis."

"Hey, Sam," Steele said. "I'm not interested in the tennis."

"He told me it didn't matter he was Deep Well. He was Deep Well, he said, who would care."

"He was right."

"What's on my mind," Pearlman said, "Walker called up this morning. Wanted to know how to get in touch with the guy."

"You called for this?"

"How'd he know I knew the guy?"

"Who knows?"

"A coincidence, you think?"

"You're a fountain of information, Sam. Better you than a phone book. That's why he called."

"The guy don't have no phone in his trailer place."

"Another reason."

"He's an old guy," Pearlman said, "but he's got a little blondie girl. How do you figure that?"

"You tell me," Steele said. "In the meantime get the hell off the phone so I can finish."

"The Deep Well thing?"

"I work for a living, Sam. After this I get to that."

"Make sure you nail it down," Pearlman said. "No loose stuff."

"Don't worry."

"You miss something, Walker will cover you like a rug."

"There's nothing to miss," Steele said. "It's what I've been telling you."

Pearlman brightened. "I'm counting on you, Bernie."

"So forget this other stuff."

"Who remembers?" Pearlman said.

The dusty Toyota was gone. Martha's clothing was probably gone, too, all traces of her removed from the mobile home. For the time being, which meant as long as Kane wanted it that way, she had disappeared off the face of the earth. Kane had people watching the mobile home, waiting for a silver Mercedes to pull up in front. But it didn't matter. Walker didn't care about it anymore. He didn't want to think about it anymore. He wanted to go to his apartment and sleep for a while and forget about everything. He waited in the cul-de-sac until Kane was inside the mobile home, then he left Forest Estates and drove into town.

He meant to stop at the *Globe* and tell Steiner he'd be back later. He wanted to get back to work on the California Connection. It seemed almost appealing, that kind of Washington story. He knew the kind of story it was; it was old-fashioned wheeling and dealing, money-grubbing, corruption in high places. It wasn't the kind of story where a former vice president drowned in a river and a young girl disappeared in Virginia. It was a story you could work on and understand as you went along and deal with sources who were what they seemed to be. Even when the story fell apart it wouldn't matter that much. There would always be another one just like it. But when he got to the *Globe* building he felt too light-headed to go in; he didn't have enough strength to park the car and ride the elevator and talk to Steiner. He drove past, taking M Street over to Wisconsin. He'd call Steiner from the apartment and then take a shower and sleep for a while. After that he'd get to work on the California Connection and try to get his life back to normal again. That was all he'd wanted before—before Harry Kane came back and the old movie started again and he was playing a role he wanted to forget—and it was all he wanted now.

When he turned into the apartment parking garage he thought about Steele. There was no sign of him on the street. When he'd left Alexandria for Sholl's Colonial and then the tennis courts in Silver Springs there had been no sign of him. Walker had been expecting him then; it was the whole point. He'd wanted to put the heat on Kane for what had happened and Steele, following him out there, was how he'd meant to do it. Seeing Walker and Kane, Steele could put it together any way he wanted. Walker would have given him a direction; he would have done that because he didn't owe anything to Kane anymore. He was done owing him. It would be up to Steele to deal with Kane, Kane with him. That had been the idea. He wanted Kane to have to sweat. Kane would be able to handle it; he would probably take pleasure in it, fooling with Bernie Steele, playing the game with him, putting him in the movie. But he wouldn't be able to hide, using Walker as his emissary. He would have to do some paying himself. Walker remembered grinding his cigarette against the Capitol steps, thinking it was an act of revenge for the vice president, getting some satisfaction from it. He'd meant it to be like that. It wouldn't matter but it was something he could do.

But Steele wasn't around then and he wasn't around now. The thin redhead with the hard hips wasn't picking up dishes in Sholl's Colonial. Walker would have savored the irony if he wasn't so tired. He'd given Steele the opening he wanted and he hadn't been there to take it. Walker would tell him that sometime and Steele wouldn't believe it. Going up in the elevator from the parking garage Walker kept thinking about the irony of the situation. It wasn't only that he was tired; he would have savored it if he didn't feel so foolish. Steele hadn't followed him to the tennis courts and it hadn't mattered. He'd put heat on Kane but not the way he intended. He hadn't known about Martha. He hadn't known anything. He hadn't known anything about anything.

In the apartment he took off his suit and loosened his tie and went down a long corridor to the bedroom. Everything was dark and cool and he didn't turn on any lights. He was holding his keys, ready to drop them on the bureau and then get the rest of his clothes off and fall into bed. He was almost to the bedroom when he stopped and then came back along the corridor. He crossed the foyer again and looked into the living room, seeing then what had finally registered in his mind. She was sitting in one of the big leather wing chairs in front of the fireplace at the far end of the room. The drapes along a glass wall were shut but there was enough light for him to see her, sitting erect in the chair, pale legs crossed at the ankles. The thought came to him again then: I don't know anything about anything.

Karen said, "Walk slowly."

The gun she was holding looked like the one Kane had used, small, snub-nosed. Her arm was extended the way his had been. The other arm, bare and pale, was resting loosely on the chair. As he came across the room the gun moved slightly, following him.

"There," she said.

He sat in the other wing chair, facing her in front of the fireplace, and she lowered the barrel of the gun, resting her arm along the skirt of a summer dress. The light coming through the drapes let him see her face now, the wheat-colored hair pulled back tightly, the eyes set close together, expressionless. The features were different but the look was the same. It was the look on the face of the other girl. He leaned back into the chair and closed his eyes. The weariness was still there but heavier now, pushing him down, solid weight hung across his shoulders. And the foolishness. *He got Mrs. Fairly,* Kane had said. *I got Martha.*

When he opened his eyes she was still there. "I got you," he said to her.

He'd liked the way she blushed, the color soft and then darkening, finally wrinkling the edges of her eyes. It was the best blush in town, and maybe the only one. He wanted to ask her about it, about how it was done, about how it could be called up on cue, but it would only be a waste of time. Then he wanted to ask her about Mrs. Fairly, about whether they had ever met before, about the conversation across the dinner table in the lodge, about standing at the edge of the river and watching her move out into the current, but it would be a waste of time, too. It would be a waste of time to ask her about the vice president and the way her eyes had moistened and the worry over whether it was a good place to write up there. The biggest waste of time would be asking her about the nights in Alexandria, about calling that up on cue, about what they had said afterward in the unguarded time before sleep came. The look on her face was the same as that on the other girl. Kane hadn't asked Martha anything on the drive into Virginia. He hadn't bothered. Walker closed his eyes again, feeling the weight pulling against his shoulders, feeling the foolishness. There was no use even looking.

After a while Karen said, "Call him." When Walker had opened his eyes and was looking at her, she said it again. "Call him. Arrange a meeting at a time and place he chooses."

"Call who?"

She raised the gun from her skirt then and he saw it kick upward and then the orange fire radiating from the barrel. There was no sound he could remember but his ears filled with pressure and then a hot sensation flared in his right shoulder. He reached for it, his shoulder pushed into the chair, expecting to feel the wetness, waiting for the pain to come. But there was nothing and then he could smell the burnt leather and see the smoke still opening out in the air. When he lifted the hand from his shoulder he saw the hole, sculpted into the leather, blackened, six inches away. He turned back toward her then, squinting, moisture filling his eyes, seeing the gun still raised from her skirt.

"Call him," she said.

He took a handkerchief from his pocket and rubbed his eyes, trying to think. He wasn't frightened. He knew he ought to be but he wasn't. *It never looks like murder,* Kane had said. If that was true she wouldn't shoot him. It would be something else. *A plausible accident. A plausible illness.* Or she would shoot him and make it seem he'd come in on a robbery, the place ransacked. She could make it seem like anything she wanted. He looked at her again, trying to find something in her face he could fasten on, some hint of what she would do. He was still looking at her when the gun shifted and kicked upward again and there was the orange fire and pressure in his ears and a searing sensation in his other shoulder and then the smoke unfolding in the air and the smell of burnt leather.

When he could see her again, see the summer dress and the wheat-colored hair and the gun raised above the skirt, he said, "There's no phone there."

"You called him before," she said. "Call him now." She was standing then, rising from the wing chair in an unbroken motion, her arm still extended toward him.

He stood up, facing her, holding his arms rigid. "He won't be there," he said.

"Then call until he is."

In the library off the living room he dialed the number Kane had put in the *Times*. He stood beside the desk, facing her. Karen had taken two steps inside the room and then stopped, keeping the distance between them, keeping her arm extended. The room was darker, blinds pulled against the sun, but he could see her better. He saw summer sandals and a pale green dress and tightly drawn hair and a scrubbed face without any touch of color and expressionless eyes. Then he was looking down at the gun, seeing the thick, squared-off barrel, knowing now she would shoot him if he didn't make the call and maybe if he did.

Kane answered on the first ring. Walker felt his legs flex and then go loose and he leaned into the desk, bracing himself against it. He looked away from her, trying to concentrate. "It's me."

"I know," Kane said.

He waited for Kane to say he'd call back from the other phone, the laundromat phone, but Kane said nothing. There was no background noise on his end of the line and none on Kane's; it was the first time they had talked that way. He tried to think what it meant, the silence, if it meant anything at all; then he thought it might be the way of alerting him, letting Kane hear the silence on Walker's end, letting him know he wasn't doing it the usual way either. If he knew Walker had also altered the procedure maybe he would know something was wrong. But Kane had said it changed everything when Walker appeared at the tennis courts. Maybe that was why Kane didn't change phones now. Maybe it was because the old procedures didn't matter anymore. Maybe it was all different now.

He waited, letting Kane hear the silence, hoping it still meant something. Then he said, "I didn't think I'd get you."

"No?"

"I didn't know where you'd be." When Kane didn't say anything Walker let him listen to the silence again. Then he saw Karen move. She took another step into the room, narrowing the distance between them. "I have to see you," he said.

Kane didn't hesitate. "All right."

"When you want."

"Then the usual."

"You sure?"

"Why not," Kane said. "For nostalgia's sake."

Walker looked at Karen, standing still now across the room, and then at the gun. He kept thinking about it but there was only one conclusion. Maybe she would shoot him no matter what he did. "You want to know what it's about?" he said, taking the chance.

"No."

If everything wasn't changed Kane would understand. He would know that unless they changed phones Walker wouldn't offer to say anything of substance over the phone. Kane had insisted on that from the start. It was how they did it. He always assumed the phones were tapped. "Okay," Walker said. He waited then, holding the phone to his ear as if the conversation was still going on, letting Kane hear the silence. He waited until Karen took another step toward him before he hung up.

After it was over there was no sound in the room. He kept leaning against the desk, still braced against it, not certain he had strength enough to move. Her arm was still extended toward him. "What do we do now?" he said finally.

"Wait," she said.

"I came back to sleep."

She moved to the side, watching him, opening the way back into the living room. "Then sleep."

He walked out of the library and slowly crossed the living room toward the fireplace, feeling her behind him, keeping the distance. He wanted to touch the furniture, balancing himself, but kept his arms tightly at his sides. When he was back in the wing chair, the weight bearing down on his shoulders, sitting with his shoulders between the two blackened bullet holes, he said to her, "We didn't say where we'd meet or when. How will you know?"

There was a flicker of movement in her eyes but her expression didn't change. The line of her mouth didn't change. "Don't flatter yourself," she said.

Giving up the mobile home was the hard part.

Martha had been a pleasant diversion but he'd known she was temporary. The idea was probably appropriated from the Soviets. Wealthy widow, young girl, Walker's playmate—stimulate a primal need was the idea. It wasn't an ineffective operating procedure, but trying it on him was hoping for a miracle.

The Soviets, give them credit, would have known that. Kane's view was that if a gift was given, accept. But he never expected it to last.

The mobile home was another matter.

He hadn't expected it to last either. It was as temporary as Martha, picked out so that when he left there would be little left behind. What he hadn't counted on was the feeling he'd developed for the place. It was efficient, unpretentious, mobile—everything, it occurred to him, he was himself. The choice his, he'd tow it to his next assignment, make it—insofar as that was possible—his permanent address. When Kane analyzed his feeling for the mobile home he wondered if it meant he'd grown older than he knew. It suggested a transition to a time when there was no new assignment, when he might be living somewhere in a place exactly like it, reading history and playing some tennis and maybe still running at night when it was cool and traffic was down. Company men never settled down that way, not if they had had an assignment once that caused irritation to a group like the repairmen, yet that was the way he found himself thinking now and then. He could only attribute it to age. He'd become attached to a long aluminum box with walls that shuddered when a door was closed, a place as temporary as he was himself. How else to explain that?

The two suitcases with his clothes were in the bedroom. They would be picked up after he left and then the mobile home gone over to remove the traces of his presence. He'd wrapped a bottle of Jameson in a towel and put it in the backpack with two plastic glasses. There was nothing else to do then. He walked back down the hallway and looked into the bedroom at the suitcases, then came back to the kitchen and stood there, adjusting the weight of the backpack. He had on his blue shorts and jersey and white knee socks and New Balance running shoes. Standing there, delaying it, was what made him wonder about his age. You could deceive yourself about it. You could know what it was and not know what it did to you. You could find yourself liking a mobile home and thinking about taking it with you. You gave in to it, it was a sort of thinking you never recovered from.

He shut the door behind him and crossed the cul-de-sac and walked down the asphalt street that led out of Forest Estates. He began to run then, taking his time, working through the stiffness and hurt always there at the start. The night was still and humid and sweat came at once. He took the route he'd taken before, keeping to the edge of the street, running through pools of yellow light from street lamps. He kept his mind on the way his legs felt, waiting to get past the beginning and find his stride, thinking about that now and not the mobile home.

He knew better than to do it, but after a while he started looking over his shoulder every now and then and looking down side streets when he crossed an intersection. There was no point to it. There was no more to see than to think about. It was why he'd been thinking about the mobile home and getting older and then thinking about his legs; thinking about those things you didn't think about things even more out of your control. When that was the situation, it was best to think about anything else; it didn't matter what as long as it blocked out the other thing. But that was always easier said than done. He didn't plan to do it and the next thing he was looking over his shoulder, seeing the dark street and the pools of yellow light he'd just come through and wondering how it looked from behind, the glow tape Martha had put on the back of his jersey. When she did that he'd known how it was meant to happen. Now it was happening and he knew he shouldn't think about it.

He thought about the houses for a while. They were bigger now than the shabby tract places around Forest Estates, aluminum-sided places set close together with big trees in front, everything dark except a shaded light now and then in an upper window. There would be a couple more blocks like that and then the houses would be brick and larger and set farther apart and he would be in the realm of mortgages you never got out from under. It would go on that way until it abruptly changed, no buffer zone between, to insurance agents and real estate people and dentists and family doctors in the big brick houses; after that the houses had been cleared away for fast-food places and then a shopping center and acres of asphalt and no center to the thing he'd ever discovered and on the other side of that were the drive-in banks and low office buildings and the parking garage he'd picked out once because it looked like every parking garage you ever saw. Why a parking garage, Walker had asked him once, and Kane had said why not. Then he'd said because it was easy to get into at night and there was plenty of room and the raw concrete amplified sounds so you wouldn't be surprised and you didn't worry about somebody at a bar stool next to you or a bug stuck somewhere. But why out here, Walker had asked him, and he'd told him it was because the longer it took to get there the easier it was to tell you were followed. Walker had seemed to accept that. After a while he got accustomed to the mystery of the place late at night, the play of dark and shadow and the sound of his footsteps on the concrete. It came to seem to him the right place for the business they had to do. Kane never told him they could have done it as well in a couple dozen other places he knew about.

Remembering that got him thinking about Walker and he thought that might get him through it. It might occupy him enough. Walker had tried to tell him on the phone and then he had the rest of the time to sweat it out. In one way he deserved it. He'd wanted to put pressure on Kane for what had happened to the vice president and now it was out of hand; that was how he'd think about it. He'd think he'd gotten into something he didn't know enough about and now it had blown up; pressure on Kane was one thing, death another. He'd agonize over it, and in one way he ought to. It might teach him something about meddling in what he didn't understand, though Kane had little faith in the capacity of reporters to learn from experience. Learn from anything. On the other hand, Walker had served him well. He couldn't forget that. Without Walker everything would have been more difficult. What he deserved was a rap on the knuckles rather than what he was going through, sweating it out, not knowing what Kane had gotten on the phone.

He was still thinking about Walker, occupying himself with that, when he saw a lighted house in the next block and cars parked at the curb, illuminated from the house. He looked back over his shoulder, seeing nothing except the dark street and the pools of light he'd come through. He looked back at the house then and knew it was what he was looking for. Closer, he could see lights on in every room, looking like a party was going on, and then he could see the windows were open, thin translucent curtains stirred by the night air, and hear music of some sort coming through them like music coming from somewhere in a waiting room. It was almost funny, a stage setting like that. The lighted party house in a dark block and then the music on top of it. He was supposed to look at the house and hear the music and maybe slow his stride; but the important thing was he would be distracted. Running by, he'd pay no attention to the cars parked at the curb in front of the house and what would come from behind.

For a moment it occurred to him he was too old for this,

then he was looking over his shoulder again, maybe first dimly hearing the sound under the music, seeing the shadows move. He kept running, keeping to the pools of light so they could see him, coming up on the house quickly now. When he looked over his shoulder he could see the blocky shape in the middle of the street, black it must be, the lights off and from the sound gathering speed. He looked back at the cars along the curb, parked bumper to bumper, knowing now how it would happen. He tried to gauge the distance with the sound building behind him, not hidden by the music if they thought that, trying to fasten on the exact place and not looking up at the magnet of the lighted house or slowing his pace. When he got to the first car he swung into the street, keeping close to the line of cars, running around the obstacle, and then the sound roared and for an instant he was thinking about the glow tape Martha had put on his jersey, thinking it wasn't exactly a bull's-eye but served the purpose. Then he could feel the heat of whatever it was and out of the corner of his eye caught a glistening fender forcing him into the line of cars and the roar filled his ears and then it was time. He drove his left foot into the asphalt and pushed off it, turning and diving to the right, twisting, hitting the hood of the car with his stomach and then pushing with his arms and flipping over like the car was a diving board without springs, banging his hips and shoulders against the metal but coming down on wet grass as whatever it was sheared away metal on the other side. He lay there a few moments, feeling his heart in his chest and the grass wet on his skin, and then the second one came by, its lights on now and the same roar and was gone in the next block.

Flat on the grass he catalogued the places it hurt and touched the most outrageous ones, feeling his hand come away sticky from both knees and one elbow and then a gash under his chin. He moved his arms and legs, seeing if anything was broken, and then knew what was. He sat up and got the backpack off but the smell was so distinct he didn't need to open the zipper. He decided to hell with it then and after a while he was able to push himself up and go up the walk to the house, realizing he was listing to one side and in the light seeing the blood on his legs and dripping down the front of the jersey. The door was open and he went inside through the bright light and found the tape player before he found the phone. He thought about seeing what the music was but then decided to hell with that too and made the call. He didn't tell them, but without the Jameson to look forward to he was too goddamn old and battered to run the rest of the way.

25

"Christ, Harry!" Walker said when he saw him.

Grimacing, Kane lowered himself to the concrete and aligned his back against the low wall. Then he asked Walker for a cigarette.

"You quit."

"I just started again."

In the house before they came for him he had cleaned up some of the blood but more had come and now it was crusted and the aching had started. He pulled the smoke into his lungs and felt the warmth, but that got him thinking again about the Jameson and how it would feel. Gentle sneaky stuff. Pain killer of preference. He told Walker about the bottle in his backpack when he started out and how it hadn't made it through. It was a goddamn shame.

"Christ, Harry!" Walker said again. There was worry in his voice but it was mixed with relief. Kane looked like hell but he was breathing. Walker was still standing, staring down at him, looking like hell himself. His shirt was open and wrinkled and his hair was flattened across his forehead. His eyes, what Kane could see of them, looked drawn from lack of sleep.

"I can't talk so far," Kane said, and motioned him down on the concrete. When Walker was there, their shoulders nearly touching, he said, "The one time we need it."

"You okay?" Walker asked him.

"The people who picked me up," Kane said, "I tell them to get a new one on the way. They said they didn't know what it was. Goddamn Anglophiles."

"For God's sake," Walker said. Then he said, "Company people brought you?"

Kane drew on the cigarette and didn't answer.

"What happened, Harry?"

He looked at Walker and could see the worry and relief on his face. With the Jameson, drinking for a while and not saying anything, Walker would relax and Kane would feel the warmth tingling down his legs and then they could talk out the rest of it. This way, there was no pleasure in it. It was just something they had to get through. Kane asked for another cigarette and lit it from the old one. Then he said, "Tell me what happened to you?"

"Karen—" Walker started to say.

"I know about that," Kane said. "She was waiting when you got back. When we took Martha out of circulation it was her turn to go to work." He paused and then said, "You let her know when you came to the tennis courts?"

"You knew about her all along?"

"When you got together," Kane said, "is when I came back. We were wondering then. When the vice president got Mrs. Fairly and I got Martha it fell into place."

"Christ, Harry!"

"It's why I checked you out first," Kane said. "That and the money. I had to make sure you didn't know about her." Then he said, "You weren't in danger, you're worrying about that. It's the unwritten rule: Never rough up a journalist. You guys are a protected species. She hooked up with you, it meant the repairmen were tired of waiting. They wanted some action. The best thing, situation like that, you don't wait around and let it go too far."

"You were using me, Harry."

"Using us all," Kane said. "You, me, the vice president—we got them to overplay their hand. Now they go back to sulking. You had a better way?"

"The vice president is dead."

"A fate we escaped," Kane said. "Look at it that way."

When Walker said nothing Kane was able to smoke and feel the warmth and then think about getting up again when he had to. The wise thing, he would have stayed on his feet, kept moving around, telling Walker that way what he had a right to know. Thinking about the Jameson had made him lower himself to the concrete. Without it he'd need Walker to get him up again.

"How'd you let her know?" he asked him again.

"I called Pearlman from her apartment. He gave me directions to the tennis courts."

Kane shook his head. "Tapped phone."

"In my place," Walker was telling him, "she didn't say anything. She just told me to call you. After that we sat in two chairs and waited. We sat there the whole time. She never even blinked. She never even changed expression. When she got a call she just walked out."

"They told her I'd left," Kane said. "It's all they wanted out of you."

"She had me fooled, Harry. I never guessed."

Kane shrugged. "They do good work now and then." Then he said, "You came here after that?"

"I didn't know what else to do. I called the number. When there wasn't an answer I drove here. I left the car by the bank. I didn't know if they were waiting for you or something had happened. I didn't know what the hell was going on. Then the car came up and you got out."

"What they had in mind," Kane said, "was a little running accident on the way. You around, they couldn't do anything here. They knew from Martha about running at night and they figured it was how I was seeing you. They got you to set it up and waited for me to leave my place."

"You knew that," Walker said, "why did you come?"

"Take more of them out of circulation. Get the rest back in hiding. The idea they had was to bump me on the street and have an item in the *Globe* about another jogger wiped out. We had some people following me and when they made the move we picked them up. I got a lift over here afterward."

"You got hurt, Harry."

"A tumble. It's when I broke the bottle." Kane took another cigarette from Walker, lit it, and told him that Karen had been picked up when she left Walker's apartment.

At first Walker didn't say anything. Then he said, "She's at the place with Martha?"

"Something like that," Kane said.

26

Walker had wanted to know the rest, so Kane told him. It didn't matter anymore what he knew. He hooked up with another woman, he handled it himself. Kane had made him famous and then come back to town and got him out of trouble so he could go on being famous. Be prepared, he used to tell him; then he'd come back to show him what it meant. It wouldn't happen again. He wouldn't be back. Walker was on his own now and it didn't matter what he knew, so there was no reason not to tell him the rest. Kane wasn't worried about it ending up in the *Globe* or a book for Pearlman. Walker did that, nobody would believe it. Walker probably wouldn't believe it himself.

First he told him the rest about the vice president. You had to remember he'd had no access to the Potomac stuff, so how did he get the information he'd passed to Kane? Back then Kane had been telling Walker the Potomac stuff went all the way to the Oval Office; he'd kept telling him and Walker had kept fighting it and then it was there in front of him. Except for one thing. There was one thing Kane had never told him. He'd kept telling him the president was involved but he'd never told him the vice president was the one leaking the Potomac stuff. And he'd never told him the vice president was getting the stuff he leaked from the president himself.

When the heat from the Potomac stuff reached the Oval Office the president had decided it was time to save his own ass.

He turned to the vice president, letting him think he was taking him into his confidence. He told him what had been going on. He made it seem he needed someone to confide in, someone he could trust, so he could think his way through the mess. He knew the vice president would leak it. That was the point. He wanted to pull the plug on the people around him. They went down, he might hang on.

Maybe the vice president had known what was going on. Nobody ever said he was dumb. They said he was a crook. For his own reasons he'd wanted to pull the plug on the same people. Of course, the president never told him about his own involvement in the cover-up. He just cried on the vice president's shoulder about the terrible things his people were doing. He got rid of them, he was hoping he'd survive himself. It was a long shot but he didn't have any other. His presidency was at stake.

Actually, Kane admired him for that—the final struggle he put up. He'd come within a hair of bringing it off. He leaked the incriminating stuff about his people to the vice president and then it was leaked to Kane and finally Walker and Bickel wrote it up in the *Globe*. After that came the resignations and indictments; the president was hurt but the idea was he could put in new people and keep going. Public sympathy started shifting his way; people began to think he was a victim of bad advice. That was when the company had stepped in.

When the vice president left office he stopped getting information from the president, yet the Potomac stuff kept coming out in the *Globe*. It was something the president never understood. He had his leak and then he closed it off by getting rid of the vice president; he never understood how he did that and the Potomac stuff still kept unraveling on him like a goddamn ball of yarn. It kept coming out in the *Globe* and then he was out of office himself and he never got it figured out.

The second thing Kane told Walker was how he learned the stuff he'd passed to Walker after the vice president was out of the picture. Actually, he hadn't needed the Potomac stuff to Walker at all; he could have passed the Potomac stuff to Walker without him. He went along with the vice president was gone he handled it himself. The vice president must have wondered about that, but he didn't think Kane had any information on his own. He must have decided the White House had sprung another leak, one he didn't know about. He didn't know about the president's fatal weakness.

The president was as interested in history as Kane, but the history he had in mind was his own. He liked to hear himself in action. He liked to savor the good lines he got off. So he put the tape equipment in the Oval Office, and when he did that it was over. It never occurred to him you could tape the tapes. Kane had had the Potomac stuff while it was happening. The president made his other mistake when he kept the tapes, thinking he could exercise executive privilege; but it wouldn't have mattered. If the courts hadn't forced disclosure the company would have used its copies against him. Kane would have passed them on to Walker. The Potomac stuff had made Walker famous, but think what it could have done if he'd produced copies of the tapes.

Then Kane asked Walker for the keys to the Mercedes. "Don't worry about it," he told him. "You'll get a call." Walker asked how he was supposed to get back to town.

"Don't worry about that either."

Kane smoked another of Walker's cigarettes. Then he asked Walker to give him a hand. He said he wasn't sure he could get up himself. When he was on his feet he kept listing to one side and grimacing as he moved, the exercise lines in his face

133

deeper now than before and blood crusted on his legs. He moved stiffly through the blue light, looking down at his running shoes to keep his balance, then came back to where Walker stood by the low wall, looking at him.

"What do you think now?" he said. "You think the repairmen might have been under orders? You think it's possible?" When Walker didn't answer Kane said, "You hear from him, he suggests it might be time for a profile, a president-out-of-office thing, I think I'd let it go. Tell him to look up Bickel."

Kane reached out and they shook hands. Then he went back through the blue light and down the ramp, listing to one side. After he was gone, Walker went down the ramp to the entrance of the parking garage, feeling like he was coming out of a movie, a movie he thought he'd seen but had turned out to be a new one, a new one he'd never heard about. He smoked a cigarette while he waited. It took about ten minutes. It looked a real cab and the black man behind the wheel lo real cabdriver. But how could he tell about an